)reigners, Drunks and Babies

__ er Robinson was born in Salford, Lancashire, in 1953
l grew up mainly in Liverpool. He has degrees from
universities of York and Cambridge. After teaching for
ny years in Japan, he returned to Europe in 2007 and is
·rently Professor of English and American Literature at
University of Reading. The poetry editor for Two Rivers
ss, author of many books of verse, translations, prose, and
rary criticism, he is married with two daughters.

T

PETER ROBINSON

Foreigners, Drunks and Babies

Eleven Stories

Two Rivers Press is represented in the UK by Inpress Ltd and
distributed by Central Books.

Cover design and illustration by Sally Castle
Text design by Nadja Guggi and typeset in Pollen

Printed and bound in Great Britain by Imprint Digital, Exeter.

ACKNOWLEDGEMENTS

An earlier version of 'Pain Control' was published on the
Brodie Press website in 2006 and 'A Mystery Murder' first
appeared in *The London Magazine* (Oct–Nov 2011), reprinted
here with kind permission. A great many family, friends,
and colleagues have helped in the writing and revising
of these stories. I warmly thank them all. And by way of
the customary disavowal, let me echo the epigraph to
'Foreigners, Drunks and Babies': 'there are no such people.'

Contents

for my family

The Academy Report

As, my Lady, you are already too aware, it was in the thirty-sixth year of the late Emperor your father's reign that the decree came down to our Academy enclave. We were debating, as I well recall, which writer should receive the annual prize in the Imperial Poetry Competition. It was a chore involving much tiresome elaboration of bogus aesthetic principles, rolled out to defend the trifling work of one or other nonentity. Yet, as all of us on the committee perfectly knew, the prize would be awarded to that poet among the three or four most prominent figures who could mysteriously summon the most threatening patronage ... The arrival of your father the Emperor's messenger from the Library on the hill above our lodgings formed a welcome interruption to those tedious deliberations. (But perhaps your ladyship will allow an old man to confess that his habit was, and has always been, to keep out of the poetry prize debate, to peruse a small scroll under the table, and lazily raise a hand when the inevitable winner had emerged as if by prestidigitation from the toppling pile of manuscript there in our midst.)

Interrupting those deliberations, as I say, was the Emperor's messenger with a request which, given the enormity and burden being placed upon our institution by his Majesty, would first astonish then utterly take us aback. Initiating what would come to be called The Great Anthology Project, our Divine Ruler thereupon required us with all due speed to survey the entire contents of the collections of verses available for sale or held in the many libraries of the Empire. We were to determine for each and every poem found therein whether it fell into the progressive or the retrograde. These were categories that, it need hardly be elaborated for your sake, were minutely specified by his late Majesty, one of the greatest writers and thinkers of this or any other age. Furthermore, after having specified to his satisfaction what exactly was to constitute a progressive or a retrograde poem, his Majesty commanded us to place a distinguishing mark alongside the title of each and every work as – dare I call it? – an Imperial instruction or warning for future generations of readers. The two distinguishing marks, to be embossed onto the paper, were, as you only too well know, a black dagger for the retrograde, and a red poppy-shaped star for the progressive.

Please forgive me if I am labouring the obvious, or, for that matter, elaborating things my Lady knows with all the wisdom and insight of her young years. Your servant is an old man, and I must beg that your Majesty forgive me if I continue to describe what occurred in my hopelessly pleonastic style. It is the only means at my disposal for keeping on at all. There were, as you are too aware, initial difficulties following out the Anthology Decree. As your father the late Emperor wrote in a language not used by ordinary mortals and, while interpreting his works was in truth one of our functions, for this once a certain friction could be sensed among our ranks about what precisely the exclusive categories covered. Moreover, it would not be too much to say that the terms themselves, when scrutinized by a hall full of sages, began to achieve a certain amorphousness of definition. Did the progressive hold exclusive claim to the adventitious and the innovative? If the retrograde were somehow shown to be resourceful, would that automatically transport it into the progressive category? And if a progressive work were also revealed to be conserving certain images from earlier poems, would this oblige it to carry the scar of a black dagger beside its title? My Lady will have already fully appreciated our difficulties without need of my numerous pedantic and painfully pedestrian examples.

Nor did it seem we were to make exception for poems that had once upon a time been hailed as progressive. No, our rule was to be applied across all provinces and for all times. Even before we had begun hiring and training a veritable army of scribes to carry out our task, there were some first signs of the dangers to come. One of our members resigned from the Academy leaving behind a letter in which he lamented the purism that sought to isolate these two (as he benightedly saw it) interdependent concepts. He further inquired whether it made sense to imagine that conserving a style could possibly mean denying it the power to evolve, or whether, for that matter, the new could carry meaning without a vital tradition in which it might be appreciated. They are indeed commonplace arguments, my Lady, but we feared to show his resignation letter to the Emperor. What became of him? The Academy has never in fact been informed of his fate, but suffice to say he disappeared. My heartfelt prayer is that he was able to take his own life in virtuous peace before the forces of correction discovered his whereabouts.

Yet a further difficulty, and one which proved in effect insurmountable, was what to do about your father the Emperor's own oeuvre. In its sustained lyrical force it is unparalleled; yet it frequently seems shadowed with memories of his Majesty's enormous reading in the anthologies of his ancestors. His works are full of instruction and sentence, informed with the wisdom of the sages, yet, presented in the highest and most purified dialect, their subtlety is sadly lost on hosts of the Empire's readers. My Lady, I hope you will allow me to take this occasion to deny categorically the ugly rumour that I know has circulated regarding his deathless compositions, namely the calumny that they were actually assembled by a committee of academicians especially selected for the task. To my knowledge, no such committee has ever existed; and, as you yourself know, the late Emperor was not one to accept advice on life-and-death matters of state, so why ever would he let the inhabitants of our frankly marginal ivory tower tell him how to attune his innermost thoughts?

Naturally, your late father's work still is – and always will be – held in the highest esteem by the Academy; but, when attempts were made by certain of my late colleagues to interpret the exclusive categories with reference to his Majesty's work, a further unforeseen difficulty arose. If, as we unanimously agreed, the Emperor's poetry would be the yardstick of the progressive, then, given that ordinary mortals were not allowed to speak in such tones, did this not imply that *all* other poetry would be consigned to the retrograde? It seemed impossible that this could be the import and purpose of the Anthology Decree.

Indeed, there was no indication in the Emperor's commands to us that his poetically inclined subjects, guided by the two categories, should not continue to draw benefit from both the innovative and the conservational. Yet one of the earliest unforeseen consequences of his instituted policy was that debates taking up vast reams of manuscript and scroll began to appear concerning which of the two types of poem the Emperor *truly* favoured – with his own verse cited and dissected in support of both camps. Indeed it wasn't long before controversies were flourishing about what type of poem best illustrated the Emperor's theories and would, therefore, be more likely to receive the accolade in the annual Imperial Competition. My earlier remarks on that yearly chore have surely underlined sufficiently the naïvety of those speculations. Yet some of them were certainly ingenious: it had been pointed out that since the Emperor was then himself the most recent in a Dynasty that has survived centuries of philistine intrigue, he instanced in his own person the flowering of the retrograde. Others proposed the case that the very unintelligibility of his verse to ordinary mortals was a mark of its being indubitably in the realm of the red poppy-shaped stars. It hardly needs adding that had either of these risible arguments reached the ears of the Emperor himself they would have been treated with a minimum of leniency in the inevitably fatal interview between pathetic tyro and divine Authority.

Yet, as you know to your sorrow, my dear Lady, the Emperor's way of life had begun to alter alarmingly some few years before he delivered (may I be allowed to suggest?) his baleful Decree. Perhaps you yourself have never been informed that he had taken to wearing a monotone monk-like garb through every season. He had further delegated all ceremonial functions to a brilliant actor who would impersonate him when visits occurred from the heads of vassal fiefdoms and the like. After begetting his only child and heir (your most forgiving Majesty), he devoted himself entirely to his studies, building for his Empress the pleasant suburban seaside villa in which you spent your quiet, yet all but fatherless childhood. As you may or may not know, he had commanded your loving mother never to set foot on pain of death in the grounds of his Library on the hill, or, for that matter, the Academy enclave on its lower slopes. There he lived with his retainers and librarians, sometimes talking late into the night with the one or two promising academicians who belonged to his sparse inner circle. Now and then vague rumours would reach us of the subjects they might treat in those nightlong conversations. At word of them, we stood abashed.

Our work continued apace, and, after some years, his cherished Academy was able to report a degree of achievement to the Emperor. We had managed to evaluate the works held in public libraries as well as most of the material then offered in the marketplace. We were already making headway with gaining access to private libraries, and had, on an ad hoc basis, you will understand, begun to standardize individual copies held by private citizens. We were not displeased to note how well the Academy had responded to these unprecedented challenges, and sincerely hoped that the Emperor would agree. Sadly, however, submitting our interim report on those labours had the opposite effect to that intended. The Emperor soon made it known to us he wished his project extended to all works announced as forthcoming from the Empire's publishing houses.

The mute and glorious departed could not, of course, object to having their verses marked with our daggers and poppies. The few living whose works were illustrious enough to be readily accessible found they were obliged to stomach the indignity without any court of appeal. But the extension of our mandate to works not quite yet available introduced a new dimension to our difficulties. Having one's verses branded with a thicket of daggers would seriously damage their reputation and, consequentially, sales. Our peaceful Academy enclave situated within the Imperial Botanic Gardens became the stage for protests by schools of young poets carrying banners and wearing various colours of helmet. When they were not trying to interrupt our efforts, they were staging pitched battles between their rival factions. It was all most unseemly. Satirical verses were circulated anonymously in which we were personally attacked. None of us escaped. Some members were physically jostled on their climb up the hill-slope towards the Library's outer gates. Cases emerged of our scribes being offered, and of receiving, bribes to increase the number of red poppies in a given slim volume. This, I fear, is what may have happened in the unfortunate case of the book thought to contain verses dedicated, with however extreme obliqueness, to your Majesty when still a budding girl. Of its luckless author's fate I'm afraid I can tell your Highness nothing.

Rumours of our difficulties at the Academy enclave reached the ears of political cliques in and around the capital. The quality of their writing in general need not concern us, even less the specific merits of their various ventures into the composition of tendentiously original folktales. What did cause rising concern at the time was the impact of their ignorance of literary refinements on the already vexed questions surrounding our work. There was quite naturally a concerted effort to associate each of the two categories with specific court factions – something which, I hasten to note, was never part of the Emperor's original definitions – thus clouding further the issues involved, and further complicating the emotions stirred by each specific adjudication.

This was bad enough, but it was aggravated by the eventual involvement of the priests who, until then, had been benignly smiling upon our efforts from their temples on the far side of the city, beyond our famous river rolling between its populous cliffs and the main thoroughfares of the markets. Taking advantage of their autonomy and elaborate structures of protection and defence, the priests weighed in on the side of the retrograde, arguing with a certain justification that the category was unfairly discriminated against. Some of their followers are, of course, utterly fanatical. There were death-threats hurled at academicians who appeared over-inclined to award red poppies. This was when my dear wife and our poor children were still with me. There were attempts on the lives of rival anthologists – not for the usual reason (one or another poet being somehow overlooked), but because they were either thought too inclined to include works bound to be garnished with a dagger, or else favour ones as likely to be stamped with a star.

Naturally these death-threats further depleted our numbers, whether because their victims went into hiding or because the threats were carried out, I do not wish to speculate. How I have survived, my Lady, I nightly ask myself among my prayers. Perhaps those years of quietly studying one of our classics under the table at the Poetry Competition debates has stood me in good stead. But word, my Lady, has recently reached me from your outer provinces beyond the White Mountains that some whose self-esteem has been so trampled by these developments are gathering supporters around them. I fear our Literary World may be descending into a vicious chaos. No, it has not happened; but I fear it. My Lady, I fear it.

Finally, your Majesty, I must compel myself to speak about the treasury. Although the monies accruing from the tax on literature are not vast, and despite a certain slight increase in public interest when the Emperor's Decree was first made public, there has been a sharp subsequent decline in revenues from the markets. One plausible explanation for this may be that the black daggers have driven readers away from certain kinds of poem while the red poppies have not succeeded in igniting an enthusiasm for other kinds. The Academy's various efforts to promote literature among the distracted populace (such as the institution of an Imperial Poetry Day) have made little real impact – beyond the inevitable one of flattering those featured poets who enjoy powerful patronage while fuelling the already smouldering resentments of those who do not. Many of the *hoi polloi* with whom I have been in any sort of contact during this difficult period have expressed their bemusement or indifference.

Admittedly, their understandings of the matter have little significance, and need not detain us here.

However, the cost to the Academy of recruiting and training scribes and clerks, the journeys undertaken through the length and breadth of the Empire, the additional expenses incurred in policing the Academy enclave and providing protection for academicians, has been nothing short of ruinous. Though requests were made to the Emperor for subventions in his declining years, it was by that stage far too late. He had turned away from the world. He was intent on the composition of his deathless cycles of last poems. It has been whispered he expired a disappointed man. Yet who could have predicted that so much misery and waste of talent would come from an effort to determine once and for all certain literary values? Who could have thought that to let such values flow with the times and to leave them in the casual care of those who need them most would prove the safer and more enlightened policy?

And thus, my Lady, it is with the most miserable regret and humble supplication that I write on behalf of those who remain in the Academy to beg your indulgence in granting our request. We most dearly beg that your Majesty temporarily suspend (should your Majesty think fit) the operation of the late Emperor your father's Anthology Decree.

Many years have now passed since I submitted the Academy's report to my Lady (who would so quickly blossom into such a fine teller of tales) and it had, I am pleased to relate, more than the desired consequence. Not only did our young Empress revoke her father's Decree; in her wisdom, she ordered us to set about removing the daggers and poppies from all the poetry collections that had been – I allow myself the liberty of a man surely on his deathbed – defaced by that meddlesome Imperial command. She even designed a scalpel-like knife, adapted from one of those used by her Court beauticians, to help us fulfill our duty to the Empire's culture. It was yet again an arduous task, once more almost bringing our long-suffering Academy to its knees, what with such considerations as the hire and control of workers travelling far and wide to undertake so menial an operation. Without an interim subvention from the Empress herself, the so-called Special Poetry Award, I am by no means sure that we would have been able to bring to completion her far more enlightened Decree.

We did our best; but let me end with a word in your ear. Should you, dear understanding reader, by chance or good fortune come across any of the very few copies that must have escaped our vigilance, be sure to treat it with the utmost care. The two or three so far surfacing in the markets for such things have been described in catalogues and leaflets, like the one I'm holding at arm's length before me, as, and I quote, 'quite literally priceless'.

Music Lessons

Mr King would soon blow full time. You can see the whistle gleaming in his hand. He puts it to his lips. Mr King's face is gaunt and wrinkled, permanently yellowed from jaundice. He was a fighter pilot in the war.

At the far end of a cindery field stretching down one side of a raised canal bank, your team is mounting its final attack. Your side's a goal down, but there's still time. You're the goalie. Sometimes you play on the wing. It's cold standing in the goalmouth. Your clogged soles suck and squelch as they lift out of the ill-drained pitch.

Inflating his cheeks, Mr King blows a single, high-pitched note and he shoos the boys off with his arms. Your stomach feels as heavy as your feet. The metal rugby boot studs clatter on flaked, subsiding flags. It'll take a bare twelve minutes to get back home.

You cross the vicarage's oval front lawn and ring its blue front door bell. Mum welcomes you back, but you've scurried right past her in the porch, and make down the hallway for the dining room. There the upright piano silently takes up its corner. You've got just half an hour.

First, the theory: taking a tram-lined exercise book from the scuffed leather case with its metal bar fastener hooked over the handles, you sit down at the dining table. The book of questions and the clean pages of staves lie cushioned on the thick brown felt, covered by a tablecloth at meal times. The felt is to save the wood from further heat rings, spills and scratches.

It will take you fifteen minutes to finish the exercises if you keep concentrated on the job. Some stewing steak, browning in the pressure-cooker, loudly sizzles. It's going to be hotpot, and you can't wait.

Counting the lines and spaces, you transpose phrases from one key to another; calculate major and minor intervals; guess the time-signatures for a few groups of notes, scratching in the bar lines, double ones at the end of each example. With no time to play over the passages, you complete the tunes by writing in resolving scales, mechanically arriving at runs of notes that dip under or hover over the tonic, sliding through a dominant seventh below, or a tone above, rising or toppling on to each final chord. You check the agreements with key and time signatures, then put the top back on the fountain pen and blot the page with a soft sheet that sustains yet another bluish ghosting of notes and other marks.

Slumping back in the chair, you snatch a moment to survey your handiwork. There are the lines of crotchets, quavers, semi-breves and minims, the clefs, rests and signatures, with here and there a crossing out or smudge. But you can't help regretting that the tails and strokes, the filled-in ovals sitting on or straddling the lines, never look so sure or evenly spaced as in the printed scores.

If only they could look right too! Closing the manuscript book and questions and returning them to the scuffed music bag brings a further sinking to the heart. Will you ever learn? But there's no time like the present, so you sit down at the piano and lift the keyboard lid. The maroon hard cover of *Hymns Ancient and Modern*, the detail from Piero della Francesca's 'Nativity' on *The Penguin Book of English Madrigals*, assorted dingy piano tutors, a bowl of fruit, and a white table lamp (which shivers distinctly at each note struck) top the dark wood box of the instrument.

Now the most likely piece lies open on the stand, the brass hooks restraining its pages. For the first time this week you study the score. Initially Miss Austin had given you Edith Horne's exercises, scales that are to familiarize fingers with the keys: the yellowed and dirt-ingrained ivory of the white notes, the more remote and less frequently visited black ones. The C above middle-C makes only a light, high, almost inaudible tinkling sound. The G below it stays down when you press it, and has to be deftly flicked level with its neighbours by a fingernail after the note has been struck. When the scales and exercises don't produce the slightest improvement in your application, you're tempted with books of tunes a boy might be expected to like: popular lyrics, light classics, film themes ... Now you're groping your way through *The Sound of Music*.

This Wednesday, as your eyes attempt to decipher the thick black towers of bass-clef chords, to co-ordinate them with the slopes and ranges of the melody, you're trying to make out through a cacophony of forgotten incidentals, unsyncopated hands, and halting rhythm, 'Doe, a deer, a female deer' – its catchy lilt and cadence; later, Herb Alpert's 'Spanish Flea'; and, with only a few minutes still to spare, 'Somewhere over the Rainbow'. But it's too late to hope for better now. You race out through the kitchen and, for Mum, let fall a loud 'Goodbye.' She'll have responded with a 'Goodbye, dear' – but too slowly for the words to reach you before you slam the back door, their sound hanging as if unwanted in the all but empty vicarage, like a cough between movements in some hushed concert hall.

You leap down the stone steps of the back door porch and feel the small cobbles of the yard through the soles of your shoes, cobbles that had rung to the hooves and wheels of the minister's horse and trap. The grille-like fodder baskets are still there in the stables where Dad parks the family's grey-green Morris Oxford. The upper floor was really once a hayloft. You'd seen the trapdoors in the ceiling above the fodder baskets where they used to push the hay. The place is strictly out of bounds.

'The floorboards aren't safe,' Dad said, 'and there's an end of it.'

The great blue double doors to the yard stand open and you walk on round the oval path of the vicarage garden. It's like a tiny racetrack made of red shale. There you and your brother would go for spins on bikes and crash, scraping your knees, which would be streaked with two kinds of red, the blood and the grit.

St Catherine's Street is unadopted, its cobbles reaching past the church gate as far as the vicarage drive, but no further, petering out into cinders, rocks, and mud. At the bottom of the street, with Mr Hill's corner shop still open for everything, you can see where the brew falls sharply to lock-ups and allotments: ramshackle planking and tarpaulin with smashed fences and overgrown plots, places for playing war with friends from school.

Rathbone's bread factory is more distant, beside the flights of locks in the canal; on the other bank, beyond its tow path, there rise the Wigan Alps, a high plateau of pale grey slag, the peaks giving this landmark its wry local name. Across these ashen tracts towards the railway lines are red brick ruins of abandoned workings, dilapidated pit-heads; their cable wheels and conveyors, corrugated iron roofs, and steel winding gear all dismantled for scrap. Only the walls of former outbuildings, stores, baths, and the offices have been left to the gangs of the surroundings, the Mount Pleasant district.

When Mum and Dad invited you boys into their bedroom one morning and told you the family was moving to a new parish in a town called Wigan where the coal mines were, you didn't want to go. It was frightening to think of living in a place covered with bottomless holes in the ground. But they'd said not to be silly: it was quite safe. Now you'd seen the curious circular walls, three times your height, with the

14

sharp glass of bottles cemented on their tops, and had been told by Hawthorne, one of the boys at school, that these were the old pits.

Not even the bravest or stupidest in the gang would climb those walls. It would be worse than falling into the canal, being sucked down, dragged under by the water rushing through the vents in the slimy green lock gates, or trapped in the mud at the bottom where brass beds and mattresses, bike frames and prams, even old pianos, all brown with rust and mud, would catch a boy's heavy feet and hold him under until, as it said in the Bible, he woke up dead.

The steps lead through a crack in the terrace next to Hawthorne's house. There are three long flights, and two main roads to cross. You always want to walk slowly, be as late as you dare, since every moment will lessen the harrowing; but gravity, which you'd done in science with Mr King, makes it hard not to go down those steps without breaking into a scamper. Dropping, as tardily as possible, you recite the terms you expect to be quizzed on. Some you'd already learned from the theory book. They were in Italian: *allegro, prestissimo, andante, vivace, con brio, molto lento, poco a poco, da capo al fine.* But there were always more of these mysterious expressions to repeat once more to the end.

With a regular beat, the soles of your shoes strike the worn stone steps, sometimes splashing in the shallow remnants of recent breaks in the weather the south Lancashire plain's been enjoying. How many times have you descended into Hell? That's what your brother Andrew calls it. And how many times will you have to rise again? A memory catches you unawares as you trip down a further flight of steps. You're about the height of a bedside table. There are grey-carpeted stairs leading to the right and a bedroom door near the top of them. It opens into a small room filled with a vast double bed. The bed has a curved utility-style veneered headboard. Lying under the covers is your dad, his head down at eye level. Someone must have told you he is ill.

There's a small round metal tin on the table near Dad's head. *Fiery-devil* it says on the tin. The lid shows a bright red dancing figure with glinting eyes and a leering mouth, a sharp toasting fork in one hand and an arrowed tail. Why do you remember that? Is it because Dad was a curate then? Perhaps you asked Mum what the tin was. 'Embrocation,' she said: something she rubs on his back. But how can something with the Devil on it make him feel better?

That was the first time you thought of your father as mortal. He was ill. He might die. Even though he was a clergyman he too could go to Hell if he were bad! How many times have you climbed those flights of steps, after promising to practise as you leave the lesson, and then let it slip as soon as you're home, so that the music case can just go and rot for another week? People could encourage you, or they could threaten. It was as though the latter, or personal dislike, or an aversion of some kind, would make you not even so much as lift a finger.

So it's with bone-idle stubbornness that you view the prospect of learning to play the piano. For six days out of seven you'll bask in that attitude. Then, for a few hours on Wednesdays, you have to sweat it out.

'You'll regret it when you're older,' Dad said. 'I never had your opportunity when I was a boy, and I regret it, bitterly.'

But why then did Mum, who had musical parents, hardly ever play?

'I love all kinds of music,' she'd say. 'If only I had more time ...'

You can't let them down, but then neither can you satisfy them, except in theory. Every six months since you were eight, without exception, you're entered for a Grade of the Royal Schools of Music exam, and without difficulty have managed five of them. Granted, you never pass with distinction, but you do get through. Then the certificates arrive in the post. Even turning up half an hour late for the most recent, mistaking the time, you still scraped through. But this tale of successes was coming to an end. Grade Five is the last you can take without any performing grades, and you've taken none. So now it's learn the piano, or no more certificates.

You reach the bottom. Crossing Darlington Street diagonally in the direction of the black-painted front door with its brass knocker struck so many times, you can feel the trepidation and sickness catch at your throat. Ringing in your ears are the musical terms you've been repeating (*rallentando, allegretto*), like charms against flight.

Passing outside, trying to beat down the emotions that will rise in you at her appearance, the door being opened to you almost now, you hear the playing of another pupil. It always shames you to notice in the confident attack, the cascade of notes, the occasional repetitions with a slight variation of stress and interpretation, the discrepancy between the pleasure it must give Miss Austin to teach Colin, and what the next hour will bring.

But it's Miss Austin's old mother who opens the door to your knock, and who, after taking the duffle coat, shows you into the sitting room where her daughter gives the music lessons. Colin is tucking the red Associated Board examination scores into his briefcase.

'Would you remind your father of the entrance fee?' Miss Austin says. 'I've entered you and forwarded the sum myself.'

'Yes, Miss Austin.'

'And you can let your parents know I'm confident you are ready for Grade Eight, Colin,' she adds.

Showing Colin out, Miss Austin motions you to sit down. While she's away in the hall, perhaps giving a few more words of encouragement to Colin, you take in the familiar surroundings. The Austins' sitting room is reserved for proper acquaintances and strangers. Their upright pianoforte has been placed on the left behind the door. On the other side, far enough along the wall to allow it to open, there stands a presentation sideboard, supporting above its laminated drawers a number of photographs of different sizes in variously elaborate frames.

One contains a picture of Miss Austin as a girl, and tucked into the corner is a small snap of her in teenage; another shows Mr and Mrs Austin together on their wedding day in the fashions of before the war; and a third is of Miss Austin herself standing next to a man of about her age and height. Behind the armchair in which you're sitting is a lamp on a tall wooden stand. A metronome contained behind the metal plate in its pyramid box is placed on the piano corner. In the net-curtained bay window, on a dark wood whatnot, a beaten brass bowl contains a flourishing double-eared cactus.

Miss Austin returns, and, closing the door, acknowledges your presence. Jane Austin is a pretty redhead with freckles over the bridge of her nose and cheekbones; she's wearing a moss-green skirt and a pale pink blouse, and wears a little makeup which may have slightly softened and faded especially from about her mouth during the day. Her features are smallish, somewhat angular. She speaks with less of an accent than you, and perhaps there's a trace of the Irish in it. Miss Austin teaches music at the St John Fisher School, and supplements her income by giving lessons to support her widowed mother. She is saving with her fiancé, a Rathbones Bakery manager, towards the day when they will be able to marry. Miss Austin plays the organ for Mass on Sundays and for weddings on Saturdays at St Mary's Church.

Smoothing her skirt behind her, Miss Austin takes her usual armchair on the other side of the electric fire. It's one of the imitation-coal types, whose glass-fibre fuel glows and flickers as an aluminium fan wheel rotates in the currents of warm air produced by the red electric bulb.

'Let's see how you've got on with the exercises, John,' is how she begins.

You hand her the manuscript book and move across to the upright dining-room chair placed beside her armchair for this purpose. Miss Austin checks through the answers quickly, pointing out occasional errors.

'Careless!' she says.

When she comes to the exercise where the student is required to complete the tune by composing a few bars, Miss Austin stands over the piano and fingers the answers you've attempted.

'Did you compose these on the piano?' she asks.

'Yes.'

'Well, why then are they so unrelated to the phrases you were given?'

'I didn't think they had to be.'

'Of course they do, John, and if you sit the Grade they won't only be looking for mechanical accuracy, but considering the answers for their melodic qualities too, as you very well know.'

Miss Austin sets some more theory exercises for homework, and continues by asking the dreaded question. 'How have you managed with the pieces we looked at last week?'

This, as you also well know, is the invitation to play them.

You place your music bag against the side of the piano, and, taking out 'Home, home on the range' as instructed, secure it to the music stand with the swivelling brass pins and think of D major.

Cupping your hands over the keys as if you were holding an orange upside down, just as you've been shown, you strike the opening chords in the treble and bass, then follow them too rapidly with the tune over the rest of the opening bar, so that there is what seems an interminable pause as your fingers in the left hand search among the remoter black notes for the sharps.

Striking the chord at the next bar's opening, the harsh dissonance produces an audible sigh from Miss Austin and the correction: 'C sharp!'

'Sorry,' you say, and glance back up at the score. 'Oh, yes.'

You try the chord again with better results; then there's another ringing silence; and so it continues into the next bar, where, like a show-jumper's horse refusing the fences, your hands lose you time at each co-ordination of the one with the other, your fingers and eyes desperately scanning the unfamiliar music for directions.

After the cowboy song, Miss Austin asks you to execute 'Doe, a deer, a female deer'.

Now she's setting the metronome on you. As the mechanism swings the weighted rod ticking back and forth, you begin to panic and sweat. Your hands dither rapidly over the notes; no time to correct the discords now, you crash to the end of the tune.

But then the peace is quickly broken into by Miss Austin saying, 'So just how much practice have you done this week?'

You're running over in your mind the much-practised answers to this expected question, when you feel your nose begin to run, and sniff.

'Very well,' says your music teacher, 'let's try the piece we've been looking at in the Grade One score.'

You feel your limbs ungainly and sticky as you reach over the side of the piano stool and into your music bag. The scores rearranged and turned down at the right page, you set off into the most rudimentary classical piece set by the Associated Board of the Royal Schools of Music for that year.

With the prospect of an exam in mind you can focus your efforts that bit more, and have actually played this piece two or three times. There are shorter pauses for note-finding, much less discord; but as your eyes and hands make their uncertain way along the staves and keys you feel your nose running again, and your sniffs begin to divide the music with almost the regularity of bar lines. Sometimes you have to sniff during rests, and the noise seems to fill the Austins' sitting room with a resonance and pitch more offensive than any discord on her pianoforte.

'Stop!' Miss Austin calls. 'Please, John, please, before you go any further, will you blow your nose?'

But you know there's no point feeling in your trouser pockets, for there is no handkerchief there.

'Don't you have a handkerchief?' Miss Austin asks, after you've sat motionless a moment.

Hot to the roots of your hair, you sheepishly shake your head, at which Miss Austin finds a square of thin white cloth from the sideboard and hands it to you.

'Now don't ever come to one of my lessons without a handkerchief again.'

You blow your nose with a brass-instrument sound.

'I don't know ... I just don't know,' Miss Austin is repeating to herself. 'I've tried everything with you, John. I've given you good tunes to play, instead of the scales and exercises my other pupils manage perfectly well with, but still you don't try. You don't want to learn to play the piano, do you?'

There is no answer, and Miss Austin needs no reply.

'You know your parents want you to learn; I've spoken to them about you, about how you just don't practise enough, don't take the instrument seriously. You're wasting your time, and you're wasting mine. I've listened to this shambles week after week, John. Haven't you ever thought how much money your parents have spent on your lessons? If you don't practise there's absolutely no point coming at all. It's a waste of your father's good money.'

Miss Austin is speechless: she has no more to say. And you can make no answer, it's true. So Miss Austin relents once again, as she's done so many times before.

'I won't set you any new pieces,' she says, more calmly now, 'but don't come back next week without preparing those you can't play, properly, mind.'

You nod, conscious that there's little else left to endure.

Her next pupil hasn't arrived yet, but Miss Austin shows you to the door. At the threshold you catch a gust of cold wind from the darkened street. It's a relief to be out into the air as the door shuts behind you. The phlegm's in your nostrils again, and you loudly sniff as you cross the road – smiling, unabashed.

❧

'Dad, would it be possible for me to give up the piano?' you ask before leaving for school one morning.

'Haven't we had this out already?'

'But Dad, I just don't seem to be improving at all.'

'And we know why that is, don't we?' he comes back.

'But I've no ear for music, Dad.'

'You know that isn't true, John; you may not have perfect pitch, like Andrew, but it's perfectly good enough.'

'Wouldn't it be a saving if I gave it up though?'

'No, it would be a waste of the money we've already spent on your lessons so far.'

'Nobody ever asked me if I wanted to learn to play the piano, anyway,' you find yourself saying in a sulky, lowered tone.

'Put that pet lip away, John, dear,' your mum says.

'Nobody asked me when I was a boy if I wanted to learn the piano,' your dad continues, 'and I regret it now. I always will. And you will too if you don't take the opportunity that's offered you. Practise more. You'll enjoy it more. And no more buts.'

'But Dad, you're always going on about how you'd like to have learnt, so why don't you?'

'Well,' Dad says, and pauses, 'it's very much more difficult to learn when you're my age. Your fingers have grown stiff. It's too late for me now, I'm afraid.'

'And I'm afraid you'll be late too, if you don't get a move on,' Mum says, rising from the breakfast table. 'Do you want another piece of toast, Bob?'

'No,' says your dad abruptly.

Your mum gets up and begins to pile the empty breakfast plates on a large wooden tray.

'So what's got into you today?' she mumbles as her husband leaves the room.

❧

It seems, however, that it isn't too late for your dad. Encouraged by your mum and the friends with whom they perform madrigals, he becomes the third member of the family to have music lessons with Miss Austin.

He practises more than you boys, finding more time from much less to spare. Where you play with a lazy hammering style, indicating, if further indication were needed, a resistance that overrides your formal submission to the routine, your dad sits at the piano with a purposeful upright posture. He exercises his fingers, and holds them carefully over the keys like a cub reporter learning to touch type. He makes steady progress over time, and seems pleased.

Each Thursday evening, a little before seven o'clock, he leaves the vicarage and walks down St Catherine's Street, stepping out firmly in the gathering dusk over the cobbles that have detached themselves from the crumbling road. He turns down the flights of steps and quickens his pace, though careful not to slip or fall.

As he passes Albert Hughes's old house, likely your dad will remember the Sunday morning he knocked on its front door immediately after early communion, when, for the first time in his years at St Catherine's, Albert hadn't been in his usual pew. Receiving no answer on repeatedly clattering the knocker in the sleeping street, and kneeling down to peer through the letterbox, he'll have seen that pure white head of hair resting at the foot of the stairs. Albert Hughes had died instantly of a heart attack, at the top, and tumbled down, so that when your dad climbed over the yard wall and broke in through the scullery window he found Albert's face fixed by rigor mortis in the squashed and flattened shape of someone asleep on a very hard surface, a shape it had never had in life, with cold blue bruising and a broken nose whose pain the people's warden of the parish had never felt.

Your dad's not the kind of vicar who likes to wear his clerical collar at all times. Of course he believes he has a calling. But there are some clergymen, he says, smiling, who even wear their dog collars in bed. At weekends and on holidays he prefers striped shirts, loose jackets, slacks, hand-knitted pullovers, and in winter a Russian-style fur hat and a Ganex mac. During the war and on into the fifties he smoked, but about the time *Go with Labour* posters appeared around the parish, he had taken to a pipe.

One summer afternoon, in search of some Mild Virginia when on holiday on the Isle of Wight, your dad had wandered into a tiny tobacconist's. You followed him some way behind, standing apart from your dad and looking round for the war comics. There weren't any. This was the wrong kind of shop.

When you entered, a curious hush had fallen on the empty premises, and then there's a whispering between the old couple behind the counter.

'It is, isn't it?' you hear the lady say.

'Mr Wilson, it's an honour to meet you. You're here on holiday? You deserve it, the job you're doing ...'

Your dad looks puzzled; then his face assumes a genial smile. You hear your father apologize for not being the great man who the tobacconists imagined had deigned to enter their humble premises. Your dad buys an extra packet of pipe cleaners, as if in compensation.

'They need new glasses,' Dad says, as you walk back towards the caravan site. 'They thought I was the prime minister, of all things.'

It was not the only thing you learned about your dad on that holiday. As the family toured the countryside thereabouts, your mum had grown restless and somehow irritated.

'Your dad's enjoying revisiting his past,' she says one afternoon.

Lance-bombardier Jones, as he then was, had been stationed in an observation post at The Needles during the Battle of Britain. He was attached to a coastal battery.

'Your dad had some floosie here,' says Mum, as if jealous of her husband's life before she knew him. 'What was she called, Bob – Gillian or Glynis or Susan, was it?'

'Hilary.'

You glance up towards the front passenger seat and see your mother take off her glasses to wipe some perspiration from her nose and eyes. Gazing at the back of her head, you're suddenly aware that she might have been someone else. Well, if she had been, so would you, wouldn't you?

'What happened, Dad? Where is she now?'

'I've no idea,' your dad says. 'I was posted to Scotland. I never saw her again.'

It rained almost every day of the two weeks you spent in that caravan, perched on a cliff above the chines and beaches beyond Freshwater. The rhythmic beating of the heavy droplets on the metal roof had driven the family to distraction. You and Andrew would grow restless after playing hand after hand of cards with Mum, then wrestle with each other for something to do.

'Fight the good fight with all thy might,' you begin to sing. 'Lay hold on life and it shall be ...'

Your dad's twenty-minute sermon at an end, the congregation getting to their feet, Mr Coleman would strike the first few organ chords. Your mum would be standing between you two boys. You find the page and, just as the hymn is about to begin, glance up at your dad in black cassock and white surplice. Your dad seems to smile, as if at peace in his mind.

There in the caravan those struggles between you and Andrew would spill the fifty-two cards all over the floor. Dad's reading a book called *Honest to God*.

'Give it a rest, boys, will you?' he asks, the first in a crescendo-ing series of requests and imperatives. Then, nothing prevailing, he would lay hold on life by the scruff of the neck and crown the pair of you.

But now, as he descends the shadowy steps, your dad's

hands are casually thrust into his sports jacket, some papers
tucked under his arm. He's wearing an Aran sweater and
mauve rowing scarf. Reaching the bottom of Burkett Bank
and crossing the larger of the two main roads, he might be
seen to knock at one of the black front doors on the far side,
down from the haulage contractors, the dental technicians,
and the handicapped people's workshop. There might still
be enough light remaining to catch a glimpse of the young
redheaded Catholic girl who lives there. She is opening the
door and inviting him in.

Under the amber streetlamps, returning by the same
route an hour or so later, your dad seems much younger
than his forty-something years. His hair is dark and wavy,
receding at the temples, and greying a little above the ears
– which some of the ladies of the parish say makes the
vicar look rather distinguished. He is slight of build, but
beginning to put on weight. His eyes are large and blue,
deep-set; he has a small, soft mouth; and, as more often
than not with the clergy these days, he's clean-shaven.

His views tend towards the liberal wing of the Church
of England, as any of his parishioners will tell you. He's
offered houseroom in his vast vicarage to unmarried girls
who've got themselves in trouble and been turned out by
their families. He's the chaplain of an institution that takes
scores of them in until the little mites have been born and
orphaned off. He mocks with his tone of voice those who hate
the sin but love the sinner. He can talk for twenty minutes
at a time about the differences between two words in the
original language of the Bible for *love*, which is a problem,
he says, because though they mean different things, unlike
the Greeks, we only have the one word for love, which is
'love'. He has given sermons on Mary Magdalene anointing
the feet of the Saviour with her precious ointment. And
once he went so far as to tell his congregation that the most

important story in the Bible is the one about the woman taken in adultery. *He that is without sin among you, let him first cast a stone.*

❧

One evening, a few months later, Jack Halsey, the vicar's warden at St Catherine's, opens the vestry door and steps inside. He has emerged from the semi-darkness of the aisle, lit only by moonlight casting faint traces of the stained glass saints onto the trodden-smooth stone that lies unevenly where mining subsidence had disturbed the church foundations. Jack blinks as he enters the glare of an electric light bulb's aureole.

Your dad's sitting at his desk, with his back to the vestry door, busy filling in the details of engaged couples on a heap of marriage certificates. Above his head two tall Norman-style Victorian windows have been slotted into the wall; but the clarity of the sky tonight is concealed by the dust that forms a skein over the small glass panes, and the iron mesh on the outside of the windows, there to thwart the vandals.

As his eyes adjust to the vestry light, Jack Halsey takes in the familiar musty surroundings in which his vicar is inscribing Christian names, surnames, professions, and parishes. On the walls above him, photographs of vicars since 1843 look on impassively as the present incumbent scribes on in their midst. The changing styles of clerical facial attitude are there displayed, or perhaps the photographer's art, which can readily be identified in their frames hung side by side on the dark brown painted stonework.

A resolute formality, whiskers or a beard, and a very fixed look have given way steadily to the slight warmth and even the ready smile of more recent men. The tints of the photographs have shifted from a faded smoky sepia, through watery greys, to the strong blacks, differentiated greys and whites in the portrait of Canon Abrahams, the previous incumbent, and there, smaller, a photograph in muted colour with *Robert Jones 1962*— inscribed beneath it.

Beside these mementoes of occupancy there is a print of Durer's silverpoint 'Hands clasped in prayer' and a soft-focus painting of a woman's profile. She is clad in a red hood.

'Hello, vicar.'

Jack Halsey announces himself in a lowered tone, conscious that his presence might startle the vicar, who has not looked up from his clerical duties.

'Hello, Jack,' echoes your dad without turning his head. 'I must get these finished before Saturday.'

Jack and his wife Eileen get on well with the vicar's family; their sons, David and Ian, are in the same classes as you and Andrew at St Catherine's Church of England School. The four of you play out together. Jack and your dad have their differences, it's true, but Eileen's husband has agreed it's a good thing for her to take up teaching again now the boys are old enough to be left, and she's wanted to so very much.

'Can I have a word with you, Bob?'

'Indeed you can.'

Your dad abandons his writing for the moment and turns his chair around to face his warden, who is standing a little uncomfortably in the dark of the doorway. Jack sits down in an adjacent chair after shutting the vestry door.

'I've had the estimates from Rushworth's,' the vicar's warden begins, 'and it seems the organ pipes alone will set us back somewhere in the region of a thousand pounds.'

'Yes,' your dad says, 'it needs doing though. The tone's distorted by the dirt, a hundred years of it I shouldn't wonder.'

'We'll meet it,' Jack says. 'The matter can be brought up at the next Parish Council meeting. Free-will offering won't be enough, though; we'll need a fellowship drive.'

'Perhaps I'll suggest we employ a professional fund-raiser.'

'You should that, vicar.'

At the oddly firm emphasis of his words, enhanced by the silence they preceded, Jack moves uneasily on the edge of his seat, his knees apart, hands clasped between them, and head somewhat lowered, not seeming either about to go or to stay.

As speechlessness reabsorbs the vestry, your dad's on the point of returning to his writing, but, seeing his warden's uneasiness, he asks, 'Is there something else, Jack?'

'It's about some things my wife's heard said, Bob,' Jack begins, 'a delicate matter, and I don't quite know how to put it. But some of the Mothers' Union and the Young Wives Group have heard a rumour and passed it on to Eileen. We don't believe it for a minute, but it is being said around the parish, vicar, and I thought I'd better let you know.'

'I'm glad you did, Jack; now, what are they saying?'

'It's quite outrageous, Bob, but they're saying that when you've been having your music lessons on Thursday evenings, that's not what you've been visiting the house for at all ...'

It takes a moment for Jack's implication to sink in.

'Oh,' your dad says, 'I see.'

'And they're saying that rather than be preached to by a ... well, you know, they'll go to All Saints. Of course, what they're fancying isn't true, I for one, and Eileen too, of course, we know it isn't, but people will talk, and it's a serious matter for the parish, and for your reputation, as well, Bob, and think of Valerie.'

'Yes,' your dad says. 'Quite.'

'What will you do?' asks Jack.

'I could say a few words from the pulpit, but that would be to acknowledge the rumour, and my parishioners would presume I'm making a denial, when there's nothing to deny; no, that won't do at all.'

'No, it won't, no.'

'And a letter in the Parish Magazine would be unsatisfactory for the very same reason.'

'Perhaps it would be best if you stopped visiting the house so regularly.'

Your dad hasn't seen this coming, and responds to it with a thoughtful nodding of his head that might seem to say he will take the advice, or think it over, or that he has already thought of this alternative himself.

'Could you let me have the figures Rushworth and Draper forwarded, Jack?' he asks, pointedly changing the subject.

'I'll drop them in on my way to work tomorrow, and now I'll leave you to your paperwork.'

'Yes, right, I'd better get on. I am glad you mentioned the matter.'

'Right you are. Goodnight then, vicar.'

❧

'Damnation,' your dad gasps beneath his breath, glancing down at the columns of couples whose confetti has been scattered across the church steps in weeks gone by, who would already have returned from their honeymoons, and, further down, the paired names whose married lives are to start come Saturday. How and when they'll end, he can't know, but plenty of them will before the grave, of that he can be sure.

Closing the book without writing any more, placing the certificates on top of the dark red binding, he stands up, puts on his coat and scarf, then, switching off the light, steps out into the churchyard, closing and locking the door behind him.

A sliver of moon in the clear night sky shines its reflected glow down onto him, onto the gravel path, the tall grasses between graves, their various styles of tomb and cross. He stands there still for a moment; then, half in darkness, begins to move on under the meshed stained glass of one of those sainted windows, and looks up at the heavens.

Now his doubting steps slow on the path between the headstones. Your dad pauses and looks to the stars. On the low churchyard walls a system of letters and numbers marks out, as on a street map, the separate burial plots. They were all of them filled long before the close of the last century but one. Your dad's eyes fall to gazing out across the roofs of his parishioners' back-to-backs. The families have prepared their evening meals. Their tables overflow with the bits and pieces. They're eating their hotpots, crowded around a large radio, or crouched in front of new black-and-white television sets.

As your dad continues between the railed-off caskets, the draped urns, plain slabs and upright stones, he ponders his calling and ministry. He has need of their trust, for without it he cannot command their confidence. He needs his place, however small, in their lives. Without it, what help can he be? A social ministry: that's how Bishop Martin described the challenges facing him. Then more and more he understands, your dad does, pausing between the graveyard and garden, that the rumours cannot be discounted. They will only grow and grow. And this is how it comes about that the music lessons stop: first your dad's, then, patience and spare cash exhausted, yours and Andrew's too.

Driving Westward

'Terrible over there, it is,' said the staff nurse, doing her duty by a nearest and dearest. Sarah was taking a breather, a break from her daughterly bedside vigil, with a cup of hot tea in her hand, standing by the ward bay's curtains.

'I was in Donegal on holiday the other year,' she said – to pass the time of a late, wet, winter Tuesday. 'We met a couple on the way to Galway ... Californians.'

'Is that a fact?' said the nurse.

The visitor took a sip of tea and let her tired eyes close. Certainly it seemed long ago and far, far away that they had taken that vacation out west to the sea. The rain would come; the rain would come ... and wash them all away..

Sarah saw herself and her boyfriend of then beside a rough stone wall, their thumbs extended, spirits played upon by feet on accelerator pedals. How they would rise when a foot did, and the car slowed. As that beige Ford had drawn into the kerb, Sarah picked up their rolled sleeping bags, and he their large frame-rucksack. Her boyfriend, in the peak of health you'd think, had run ahead of her towards the stopping car. Wearing a bright-coloured silk headscarf, the woman in the passenger seat had wound her window down.

'We're heading for Ballyshannon,' the boyfriend said, though they were in fact hoping to reach a village not far from Galway City.

'Just hop in,' the woman replied. 'We'll take you a way down the road.'

The driver and his passenger were in what seemed to Sarah like late middle age.

'My name's Freddie,' the passenger said, 'and this is my husband – Arthur.'

'Tim,' said her boyfriend, 'and Sarah.'

'What a lovely Biblical name!' Freddie exclaimed, and Sarah wondered if she meant Tim's or her own.

Arthur was accelerating the little English car they had hired. Freddie had taken a guidebook out of the glove compartment, and began to read aloud.

'There one may imbibe', she read, 'the all-pervading mists of the Celtic mythology ...'

'You don't mind, do you?' asked Freddie, interrupting herself and addressing their two hitchhikers.

'No, not at all,' said Sarah for them both.

So Freddie began again: '... the Celtic mythology barely suppressed beneath a thinnest veneer of Christianity, as, for example, in the stone crosses of County Sligo, the landscape of Ireland's greatest poet and mystic, William Butler Yeats.'

Arthur was wearing a tweed hat that he'd bought, he would tell them, in Donegal. He was a large man, thick-necked, his casual wardrobe predominantly check. Freddie was thin, very thin. Her hair, if it was her hair, had kept much of its colour, but the face was deeply lined, the nose beaked.

She had put her guidebook down a moment now their car neared the outskirts of Ballyshannon.

'Which route will you take from here?' asked Sarah.

Arthur and Freddie were free as birds, they said, and could go any route they pleased. They had it in mind to head, it seemed, for Galway City.

'Oh,' said Sarah, hinting, 'we've rented a cottage just north of there.'

'Lucky coincidence,' Arthur was saying. 'We'd be glad to share our journey there with you young people, wouldn't we, hon?'

Divided by its river, the town of Ballyshannon sprawled across steep slopes near its estuary mouth. A bridge connected the two sides, the two countries. On the southern bank a Garda checkpoint was slowing traffic down. Below them, dark waters churned into the Atlantic breakers. A church, high above them, crested the northern hill. Since a small bridge further upstream had been blown just a few months before, this crossing was now the only road connecting County Sligo through Leitrim to Donegal. A strategic point, it was, in the campaign against the Provos. By means of strict searches the influx of arms into the sole county of Eire north of the river Erne could be significantly reduced. The Provos' training bases and jumping off points in the Republic might then be strangled. That was the idea. Bridget Rose Dugdale herself had been familiarized and briefed in Donegal.

The hired car descended a steep main street running south to the bridge. Freddie had taken up her guide-book again: '... and the old Celtic Twilight of cottage and curragh ...'

Sarah began to sense that Arthur might just be a little bit irritated at the strain of his wife's hoarse voice. It was thin, low, and slightly parched – an invalid's voice, so Sarah imagined.

Arthur was quiet at the wheel, his eyes never glancing from the road.

'Your cute little lanes just scare the hell out of me,' he said, 'and these toy-town English cars, how do you ever stretch out and relax?'

Freddie hardly seemed to notice her husband's difficulties. She would stare out animatedly, gazing and scanning across the windscreen, then read a little more from her book.

At the vistas of stone-walled plains stretching to the horizon's mountains, clouds in convoy under-lit from the Atlantic, Sarah could feel her spirits lift – as if she too were washed and refreshed by shafts of sunlight breaking through those clouds beyond the river Erne.

'Oh, look right here. It's so beautiful!' Freddie exclaimed. 'Now, Arthur, can't we stop and take a photo?'

In Bundoran, though, there was nothing picturesque to stop for. The road was high-cambered and some lumps of tarmac had cracked and fallen off from each side. Arthur sped on through, gusts hitting the car, blustery, fierce from the ocean. Pastel shades of the house paint daub had faded to a washed-out pallor. The woodwork of window frames, lintels and doors had swollen, cracked, the colour peeled away. Sarah suddenly remembered a family holiday in Aberdovey, when she was five years old, crying as she clutched at her mother's skirts. They were locked out of the holiday boarding house from ten in the morning till six at night. Sarah's tears were lost amidst the rain that soaked her face. That was the weather for bingo and penny arcades, places they would never go, thought Sarah all those years later. On rainy days the men would make a killing.

Out in the open lake country, the sea to their right, mountains were rising steeply to the left of the road.

'That must be Ben Bulben,' Freddie would speculate at every other turn. 'We're planning to do a pilgrimage to Yeats's grave,' she said.

Now Freddie was talking about the publishers Allen and Unwin. She had approached them with a manuscript. They had been civil enough to reply by return of post.

So Freddie was a writer!

Sarah was wondering what kind of books she wrote, and whether she ought to have heard of her.

In Drumcliffe churchyard, under Ben Bulben, Freddie's dependence on her husband became yet more obvious to Sarah.

'Don't forget to take your tablets, hon,' he said. 'You know how forgetful you're getting.'

'It's my veins. I have very weak veins from the course of medication,' Freddie had turned to Sarah and explained. She could feel herself adopting her friendly, concerned face as she listened.

The sky was overcast, but there was light enough for a photograph, so Arthur posed Freddie beside the stone with its proud, defiant phrase:

Cast a cold eye
On life, on death ...

Sarah read it out under her breath, and tried to imagine herself doing just that.

'His wife had a man's name too,' Tim said. 'George heard voices.'

Sarah was staring at the headstone, feeling some intangible hollowness in this pilgrimage to the final resting place of an illustrious corpse. Did she expect some ghostly visitation? There was simply the rustling of branches up above them.

'Won't you look at his check pants – a typical American, isn't he?' Freddie was saying as Arthur splayed his legs and rocked forward to take the shot.

Sarah and Tim looked momentarily nonplussed.

'Do you know why golfing trousers have such loud checks?' Tim asked.

'No, I don't know why golfing trousers have loud checks. Why do they?' Sarah said in a singsong voice, to show she knew it was a joke.

'So the balls can see the golfers in the rough!'

'Where did you get that one,' she asked her then boyfriend, 'from a lolly-ice stick?'

'Why, that's good,' said Freddie. 'Just come and listen to this, Arthur dear.' And she repeated the joke.

The Yeats Tavern would provide them with some light refreshments. A family of tinkers had encamped in the yard of that bar across the road. Freddie was imagining for their benefit the carefree life those travelling people must be leading. She was describing to Sarah the caravan they'd overtaken earlier that morning, brightly painted and gay.

'One thing I can't meet halfway,' said Arthur, 'and that is laziness. Bums, I call them. Bums.' Arthur was ordering some sandwiches and beer from the bar. Sarah helped him carry them over to where Freddie and her boyfriend were sitting in an alcove.

Above their heads, where they consumed the food, there hung a really garish painting. It showed the snowy-haired, monocle-wearing poet in a composite landscape of symbolic towers, mountains, roses, swords, mists, and swans ...

'The ceremony of innocence,' said Freddie, and began to tell them about her daughter.

Yes, Arthur and Freddie had a daughter too. Nancy, it turned out, was an aspirant poet. Right now she was taking an MFA at Stanford University. Freddie had to explain for the benefit of their English acquaintants what those initials stood for.

'Like a creative writing course,' she said.

Some of Nancy's work had been published in the little magazines.

When Freddie asked Sarah and Tim if they wrote too, all Sarah could do was wince inwardly at the thought of her boyfriend's scorn as, flicking through a school exercise book she used for recipes, he found two poems she'd composed at school, plus a sonnet to him when they first got together, and where she had copied out Louis MacNeice's 'Thalassa' in her neatest hand.

'"Our end is life. Put out to sea." What's that supposed to mean?' he said.

'Well, either you are or you're not,' said Freddie firmly, after Tim shook his head and Sarah simply shrugged.

Back in the car, they were crossing a moor with low ridges of rich brown-striated green. Groups of men with shovels were loading the dried bits of what looked like turf on the backs of trucks. Arthur was saying that if an American firm were to move in they would develop a machine to express the moisture, so as to transport the turf, packaged, in handy brickettes – and sell it back to the farmers. Everyone laughed at the very idea.

Further on down the road, Arthur told them the story of Ben Franklin in London, how he didn't go out drinking with his associates, but, rather, calculated exactly the wastage of hours for self-improvement and financial betterment incurred by their merrymaking. Time is money. That's what he'd said. Time is money. But now Arthur and Freddie were taking a holiday ... before it's too late, thought Sarah.

'Some people say he was a real stuffed shirt, Ben Franklin, but I say he was some smart guy.'

So how did Arthur make his money? It turned out he was a professor of business studies. Invited over by Queen's University, Belfast, to give a lecture series on sound investment practices, he had brought his wife with him for the vacation they would take afterwards. Freddie was hoping to pay a visit to Allen and Unwin's offices on her way back through London to the States.

Now a crossroads in the distance seemed blocked with trucks and vans. Livestock straggled off to left and right. Boys with dogs were trying to stop the flocks straying towards lake edges nearby. In Maam Cross it was market day.

'Gee, Arthur, we have to stop ... We have to get a picture of this!'

But of course they would, and Arthur was also in need

of the comfort station. He entered the general store and bar of Maam Cross's one public building, a hotel that catered for the local gentry.

Freddie was telling Sarah that the mountains of the West of Ireland were so fine and the light through clouds so lovely as it flitted over the fields, so fleeting, that she despaired of ever capturing it in words. She would love to put the place into a book.

'I've just finished reading *Watership Down*,' she was saying. 'Richard Adams is such a fine writer. Have you read him? No? You really should!'

Arthur and Tim were returning from the hostelry.

'Now, that camera of mine's in the trunk,' he reminded himself.

Opening the car boot, he took from his jacket laid across the luggage there an extremely compact black oblong.

'They're a new line,' he was saying to Tim, 'a recent development – cartridge load, self-focus, not on the market yet. How did I get one? I did some research for the outfit that makes them. What kind of shot do you want of this, honey?'

'How about one of those sheep,' his wife replied.

A huddle of long-fleeced muddy ewes, white with a jumble of black heads and legs, had just huddled their way into the square glass space of Arthur's viewfinder. It was like a flat arrowhead advancing, just below the centre line. Freddie said she loved the idea of their warmth. They were such quiet, unaggressive creatures – domesticated, tender, like a gentle human nature ought to be.

A boy in late teenage was driving the sheep towards a lorry with slatted sides for livestock transportation. Two types of buyer were circulating among the local men. There were reps from industrial combines, stud farms and distributors. Then there were the city men in small vans, bidding against the country gents. These were men in well-made brown leather shoes, tweeds, with flat or, occasionally, deerstalker hats.

'It's been a bad year for them,' Tim said from nowhere. 'Many of the farmers have sons who work in the English motor towns. The children hereabouts move away young.'

But now Sarah's boyfriend was approaching one of those buyers, a rep from some firm, as he settled on a price. He was neat and trim, wore office clothes, conspicuous green Wellington boots with his trousers tucked inside. The farmer with whom he was dealing looked more of a piece. He was leaning upon a gnarled stick, smoking and spitting on the tarmac. The buyer had nodded an affirmative to Tim's hesitant request. Sarah turned and bid farewell to the generous American couple. They had brought those sweet English people as far as they were going down that road. The buyer was opening the doors of his car, gesturing to the young hitchhikers, his purchase being loaded on a truck nearby.

Arthur had his picture, Freddie her memories. Carried away in that mud-bespattered transport, Sarah looked behind to see Freddie and Arthur standing side by side: her cream raincoat and headscarf, his bright checks amongst the brown and grey of the country people. Freddie was pointing at a man on horseback. Arthur raised the small black box to his eye. Then they were lost forever.

Sarah sighed and took another sip of her quickly cooling tea.

'Terrible over there, I was saying,' said the nurse.

'Yes,' said Sarah. 'I'm sorry.'

Then to make up for her inattention, Sarah recalled how on their way to Donegal they'd been picked up in heavy rain by a man who took pity on them right near the border. He said he wouldn't normally give lifts to people, and especially so close to the North, because the Provos had been hijacking cars, forcing drivers to cross over, then abandoning the vehicles packed with explosives.

'Yes, I heard so,' the nurse said. 'I know some people who were born, brought up, and lived all their lives right near the border. But they were so frightened about what could happen they decided to up sticks and flit to Dublin. And do you know, the day they moved was the very one some faction or other chose for their outrage in O'Connell Street. They had only that minute stepped off the bus and were blown to smithereens.'

'How terrible,' Sarah said.

'It is that,' said the nurse, 'but, then, everyone over there has a story like that they can tell.'

Lunch with M

There was a chilly breeze blowing across the London Transport bus station, gusting its flurries of drizzle. The bus to Harrow was empty. I dumped my luggage on the seat beside me, sitting towards the back above a wheel. Through suburbs under flight paths the bus route led, the jumbos descending to disappear behind roofs of semis. House doors and windows were still the traditional inter-war green, allotments visible between them. I settled down into the slightly reverberating seat to savour my return as the bus came trundling to a halt. It was home time, just after four: we'd pulled up before a comprehensive school's gates. Out poured a swarm of school kids in bits of uniform. Shouting and laughing, they pushed through the door by the driver, piling up the stairs, or into what remaining seats there were. Their bags and satchels were covered in the names of latest groups, boy- and girlfriends' linked nicknames. They were calling out in-jokes, making sarcastic comments, crowding into their small cabals.

'Move along the bus, please,' the driver called.

Two girls on the seat in front began singing snatches of a new hit song. An old man sat near me glanced round as if to say, 'Young people!' I recognized his look and smiled. The younger generation had ruffled his earned composure. The younger generation ... ah, when do you realize you're no longer part of it? The man's brief frown and my smile of agreement had forged a bond about the young. Almost old enough to be their father, here it was again: the anxiety that would grip me as the bus home from school stopped outside the local comp.

It was all a long time ago, though, and those present waves of children were pushing and shoving each other in fun, upsetting the pensioner with their loud and competitive talk: 'Oh, did he?' 'Disgusting!' 'Well, you know, she told me so.' 'I'd tell him where to stuff it if he did that to me.'

So this was home. Its English tones were only too intelligibly moving something in me once again. They penetrated there and recalled old quarrels, other distant violence done. The girls at school would fight like this, form groups to isolate one or another of their number, trying to recruit the boys into their conspiracies.

The bus had arrived in Hanworth shopping centre. Young mothers burdened with folded pushchairs, children and loaded carrier bags were taking the place of those kids who had got off. A child on the seat in front stood facing over the rest gripping its metal rim, smiling into my face. I smiled back. The mother, noticing, glanced round suspiciously. Never talk to strangers: mum warmed us over and over. I was carrying the present in my luggage. How old would May be now? Just over three and a half, I guessed.

Beyond Hanworth, approaching Hampden, the avenues grew more thickly tree-lined, the houses larger, set back from the road. The bus swung by a community hall, a tennis club, and then came the side roads bearing names of poets. Here was Wordsworth Grove. Not far ahead would be Hampden station, its level crossing gates beside the road. My stop was the one before it. I glimpsed it in the distance, said, 'Excuse me,' and started to clamber out with my luggage, the items still tagged with labels and stickers from security checks and baggage reclaim. I rang the bell. The bus came to a halt. There I was alone among the rows of large Edwardian houses. No, this wasn't right. I'd got off a stop too early.

❧

Mike's was a townhouse in a close. No fence divided the pavement from its little lawn, a tiny patch of garden leading to a maroon front door. The garage door was lifted beside it. Sally's white Metro had been parked in front, Mike's grey Renault at the kerb. I was well over three hours late. Missing the nearest bus stop meant I had walked the last quarter of a mile.

Only a few steps from my brother's front door, I saw, almost reaching out to ring the bell, Mike appearing in the entrance hall. He was visible behind the stippled glass: slightly taller than me, with a pointed red beard and thick wavy hair where mine's blond. He opened the door.

'What time do you call this? Where've you been? We were expecting you for lunch. We decided we couldn't wait any longer. It's all been eaten. Where have you been?'

'You'll never guess what happened ...'

'What?' said Mike without a smile.

'The plane was delayed,' I said, disliking the sound of my own voice. 'They thought there might have been a bomb on board at Pisa.'

'You should have rung us from the airport. We've been worried sick. I was just about to contact the police. Why can't you be a bit more considerate? You must have known we'd be worried to death.'

Only the family would talk to me like this.

'Well, you should have guessed the plane was late. I mean, it does happen quite frequently, doesn't it?'

Mike stared blankly. I glanced away thinking that he wouldn't let me into the house.

'Come in. Come in, then, seeing as you're here,' he said.

Sally was wiping some food from May's face.

'I'm sorry,' she said. I didn't know what for.

'You'll have to make do with a bacon sandwich,' Mike said, attempting to alter his tone. 'We don't have anything planned for supper.'

Were they apologizing for eating the lunch without me?

'Anything's fine. I'm not very hungry,' I lied. 'A bacon sandwich is fine.'

'We've put you downstairs in the garden room,' said Sally. 'May is in the spare room now. May, say "Hello" to your Uncle George.'

May shrank back towards her mother's calves. She looked up at me. Perhaps she was trying to remember if she'd seen me before.

'Hello, May,' I said. 'Haven't you grown! How old are you now?'

'I'm nearly four, aren't I, Daddy?'

'You're three and a half,' said Mike. 'Your birthday's not till next September.'

May seemed about to countermand the facts of her birth.

'I've brought you a present from Italy,' I said. 'Do you want to see what it is?'

May looked up towards her father.

'I think perhaps you'd better have your bath and get ready for bed, then Uncle George can show you his present.'

'Fair enough,' I said, supporting Mike. 'If you're a good girl and be quick then we can see what it is.'

'You know what it is, Uncle George.'

I was about to reply that I knew I did, but it was a figure of speech, when Sally took hold of May's hand and began to lead her up the stairs.

'Shall I take my bags down?' I asked. 'It'll get them out of the way.'

'Why not,' Mike called as he disappeared into the kitchen.

The garden room, as its name suggested, let out into the back. My brother and his wife had made some changes since last I visited. Hung on the walls above the divan were some of my brother's old pictures. At school he had been a keen painter. Scientific research had pushed that to the back of his mind. Instead of deep-shadowed portraits and still lifes in which family members figured in images reminiscent of Caravaggio-like music parties or Dutch interiors, he

46

had made holograms. The return to public display of these pictures from his school days suggested some changes of mood or attitude. But what?

Back in the hallway, picking up my travelling bags, I noticed another addition to the decorations. Mike had taken, or been given, a selection of photographs from Mother's collection. He had mounted them together inside a large frame. It was a collage of our shared childhood. I stared into a past of black and white or faded colour. There was my brother buried up to his neck in sand on Blackpool beach. Here were the two of us kneeling by a fishpond in a park somewhere, Mum above us pointing into the water at a fish, perhaps, Mike with a model plane, me holding a little yacht. Here we were in our cub uniforms. Mike's class photograph from primary school was next to it: he was the painfully thin one, with the mop of hair, sticking up at the crown, sitting cross-legged on a mat at one end of the front row.

'Remember this?' my brother asked. He was pointing towards an old photo of the two of us on the observation balcony at Manchester airport. Mike had a small black Kodak Brownie camera round his neck. I was carrying a reference book on civil aviation.

'How old do you think we were back then?' I wondered.

'Eight or nine, I suppose,' said Mike.

It will have been about then I asked myself why we'd been born English. A South East Asian family had moved into the neighbourhood. One of their children was in the same class as me. Perhaps it was because of the Sunday school visits from missionaries in Africa, their photographs of the poor black kids. Why was I not one of them? Why was I born English? That question was not far from asking why I was born at all. Mike said he could recall asking where we came from, and remembered being puzzled by the vague biological reply. He said he remembered sitting on the side of the bed wondering how it was he got out of Mummy's tummy. There would have to be some kind of a door. Despite his beliefs, Dad would never have told us that we were born, and born English, because God willed it. Why were we born English? It is, of course, a provincial question, one of an infinite series of other childish 'whys' and replies, supposing a will beyond the human, a will that also informed the creation of Englishness, England, and a destiny to go with it. Yes, but the creation of England and Englishness can be explained by recourse to history and geography – but why we happened to belong to that story could not.

∾

'Look, here's Uncle George. He's got your present,' Sally was saying to May as they came down the stairs. 'Why don't you ask him if you can see your present now?'

'Uncle George, can I see my present now?'

I made to go and bring it from the garden room. But before I could take a step, my big brother had spoken out sharply.

'Is that any way to ask, May? You won't get anything if you don't ask properly. Ask your Uncle George, only this time nicely. Now say "please" properly.'

'Can I have my present now, Uncle George, please?'

'Yes, of course you can, May,' and I went to find it from downstairs.

'Here it is,' I said. 'It's come all the way from Italy.'

From behind my back I revealed a basket made of woven reeds and lacquered to form a stiff case. It had small handles on the top, and a simple bamboo fastener. I gave it to May.

'This is to take your things on holiday,' I said. 'Why don't you see if there's anything inside?'

May was having some trouble with the fastener. Sally helped her. Out of the bag fell a small white T-shirt. May looked bemused and unimpressed as Sally held up the garment to see what was written on it in bright red letters.

'Say "thank you" to Uncle George,' said Sally.

'Thank you, Uncle George,' my little niece said, rather woodenly.

'What does the writing say?' asked Mike, as Sally turned the T-shirt front towards him. '*Avanti popolo!* What does it mean? Is it a Ferrari advert?'

'It means: "Forward the people",' I said. 'It's a slogan, a socialist rallying cry.'

'Oh, is it, indeed,' said Mike. 'And you think it's a good idea for May to go round Hampden wearing a piece of Bolshie propaganda?'

I wasn't quite sure if my brother was joking.

'No one hereabouts will know what it means,' said Sally, placating her husband. 'I don't suppose it's going to cause a political storm at the play group.'

'OK, OK,' said Mike. 'Let's make May a bedtime drink. And I suppose you're ready for that bacon sandwich now.'

❧

Those visits to my brother's house were always like walking on eggshells.

'Just put the croissants on now and bring them in here when they're ready!'

It was Mike's voice, abrupt and dismissive from behind that morning's *Sunday Times*. I looked up to see Sally's face freeze into a mask of disbelief. She turned and disappeared round the wall into the kitchen.

'I only asked where we should eat breakfast,' she muttered.

No, there doesn't ever seem to have been a time when

we weren't competing, when we somehow didn't quite get on. But that was only to be expected. Sibling rivalry, Mum would say, and leave it at that. Yet even if I didn't exactly like Mike, I did love him, and he would always be my brother.

There was no conversation for a while as we sat together in the living room, munching the croissants Sally had brought through, and studying the Sunday papers. They were all still full of it: 'Pub incident that exposed a spymaster' ... 'How MI5 forged bank accounts in bid to smear MPs' ...

Behind his paper Mike was engrossed in the leader. I was glancing down the columns and over at the photo of the spymaster's gravestone in a Derbyshire churchyard. *The Sunday Times* had a close up of his face. It was the photograph published in the mid-1970s, the one that revealed M's identity as head of MI6.

Beside the blurry image were clearer ones of Guy Burgess and Anthony Blunt. *The Observer* had 'The Secrets Spread by Smiley's People'. Beside it was a picture of M with his mother and sister after receiving a CMB at Buckingham Palace in 1964. There were smaller snaps of Sir Robert Armstrong and Lord Rothschild. The paragraph heads stood out like sore thumbs: '"My Dear Boy"', 'Defamatory', 'Spanish Waiters'. It was the same in *The Sunday Telegraph* – a photo of M in mid-conversation, his eyes twinkling behind the horn-rimmed glasses, mouth lifting into a smile, right hand index finger raised perhaps to emphasize a point. 'Spymaster's fall from grace' read the headline.

'Amazing to think we had lunch with him,' said Mike, resting the newspaper flat across his knees.

'I know,' I said, remembering.

❧

Mike had suggested we meet up beforehand at the entrance to the Pimlico Tube. He was waiting in diffused sunlight, there as I arrived, his then shoulder-length red hair and pointed beard in need of a trim. We set off to cover the short distance to the address Dad had given on the phone. It was only a five-minute walk. There was an intercom above its doorbell where we were to identify ourselves. Mike had asked if we needed our passports.

'It's not an Ealing comedy,' Dad replied, 'more a spy coming in from the cold.'

Now Mike was leaning his ear towards the intercom, fretting that he wouldn't catch the voice within, the voice behind the pale stone façade of buildings in such a posh part of London. At least there wasn't any traffic in this residential street just a minute or two after eleven o'clock, a Saturday morning in springtime, more than a decade back now.

'I felt completely overawed,' Mike said, 'at the thought of meeting such a very important person.'

There was a clicking sound in the door. It opened to allow us through that front entrance into a vestibule with another locked door before us. Once it was opened from within, we found ourselves facing a steep flight of stairs that made a sharp turn to the right at the top. There, at the head of the stairwell, stood M himself. He was short, on the plump side, a nondescript man in a pair of grey flannel trousers and brown suede Hush Puppies. His round, puffy face was as expressionless as you could wish for, but with bright eyes enlarged behind the lenses of his spectacles.

He welcomed us into the living room of his oddly small flat, gesturing towards the sofa. M asked if we'd like something to drink. Neither one of us had the slightest idea about how to behave back then, but Mike asked for coffee, which seemed like the right thing to say. M disappeared down the narrow corridor into his kitchenette, coming back after a while with two cups on a tray, a little jug of milk and some sugar in paper sachets. I'd been scanning his leather-bound volumes of local history from the Peak District, wedged into the bookshelf beside his collection of recent hardback literary fiction.

I needn't have worried about the conversation. Mike's decidedly more talkative, and had come along with an agenda of things to say. In any case, M had much to talk about too. He began by reminiscing about his graduate student days before the war, remembering how he and Dad had been at our age. That's where they'd met: Dad, a newly employed junior librarian, would bring him documents and rare books from the archives. He could see the family resemblance, M said, though Dad had been even slimmer than we were back then. There hadn't been a great deal to eat in Grandma's family through those inter-war years.

They'd lost touch, he said, not long after Dad had been called up.

'But I made it my business to keep an eye out for Tommy,' said M, referring to our father by a name we hadn't heard used since Grandma died. This was much easier, said M, when Dad left the Gunners and joined the Signals – the Intelligence Corps.

'I always knew where your father was and what he was up to,' said M.

M had been travelling and showed us his holiday snaps from Beirut and Israel. Yes, he had to admit he'd lost track of Tommy after he went back into the university library; but he did know of his marrying and having children. There hadn't been the occasion to keep in touch, but now that Dad was approaching retirement, M had thought to renew the acquaintance for old time's sake and expressed a desire to meet his friend's sons. Which is why we were perched on his sofa, both of us feeling faintly taken aback that such a person had been following the career of an

NCO in the I-Corps, now a redbrick university librarian in his mid-fifties.

After we finished our coffee, M picked up the phone beside his armchair and called for a car. It would arrive almost immediately. So we were ushered out of that tiny living room back down the corridor and stairs. Going out through the vestibule, M opened another door on the left and spoke to a man sitting at a console with closed-circuit television screens in front of him. He was taking his young guests to lunch and would be away for a couple of hours at most. I could see from this glimpse into his security arrangements that not only was there an intercom to identify visitors, but also a camera at head-height in the wall, and another perpetually scanning the street outside. In its screen I could see that the large black limousine, which would take us to his chosen restaurant, had already arrived.

'Don't you think it was a bit unprofessional to be showing off his surveillance devices to a couple of young strangers?' I had wondered.

'Very underplayed, of course,' said Mike, 'but doubtless effective protection.'

❧

Yet why had the head of MI6 wanted to meet us, a provincial librarian's half-couth sons, in his guarded service flat? It was a question neither Mike nor I could answer. Yes, M had known Dad before the war – a slim, weak-looking, baby-faced boy, unsuited to manual work, growing up in the precarious climate of the inter-war years. Book stacks had seemed the safest place for him. So, at the time of Munich, he was cataloguing Puritan pamphlets, writing out the file-cards by hand. M was engrossed in post-graduate research on something about mediaeval history. I imagined them meeting for the first time across a polished wood access window, M handing Tommy a reader's request slip. It might have been September '38. He'd been introduced to M's professor at the university. 'And just what do *you* know about mediaeval manuscripts?' older colleagues from the library mysteriously asked him.

Dad reached the right age in March 1940 and so was conscripted. He went into the artillery, his post held over for the duration. Never having spent a night away from the family's terrace house, he had suffered from dreadful homesickness. During the Battle of Britain Dad was part of an anti-aircraft battery stationed near St Just in Cornwall. Out of sheer boredom down there, he decided to transfer to the Army Air Corps, where he would volunteer to fly. Piloting unarmed Lysanders into Occupied Europe by night, he would drop and pick up liaison officers working with the French Resistance. 'You'll be killed,' Grandma said, and again she got her way. So it was the Intelligence Corps. Dad's searchlight battery was later converted to anti-tank guns for the invasion of Europe, his old comrades decimated in the Normandy beachhead. If Dad had learnt to fly or stayed in the artillery, we would never have been born. Mike and I owed our very existence to Grandma's maternal possessiveness and Dad's bolshie boredom with the rigid disciplinary routines of a fighting regiment.

So the war had come and dispersed many friendships. It took M out of mediaeval history and into Intelligence proper. It killed Dad's best friend, William Dixon. He was the vicar's son at Holy Trinity, where Dad sang in the choir. It was one of those terrible accidents of war. A convinced pacifist, he decided, as the war dragged on, that the proper thing to do, even for one of his convictions, was to contribute to ending it. He volunteered for the Royal Engineers. They were unloading something from a transporter somewhere in Northern France. It had tipped over and crushed him: one of the innumerable, heart-rending, pointless deaths wars cause. On Dad's bookshelves was an anthology, *The Modern Poet*, edited by Gwendolen Murphy, which Will had given to Tommy at Christmas 1941. It had come down to us from a lost, an irrecoverable world.

Dad's medals were kept in a dressing table drawer among his socks and ties. There was the Italy Star, with oak leaves. That meant he'd been mentioned in dispatches. It was for working round the clock interpreting captured German maps. When Mike and I were boys, he still had his language learning books from that time: a strictly limited vocabulary of German compound nouns soon to be consigned to the small print of military history. I imagined him in his tent through the winter rains of '44, under a mosquito net in olive groves, or on the slopes of Monte Cassino months after the battle had ended. *Et in arcadia ego* ... but he had fallen ill with jaundice and malaria. It was why he never gave blood, as Mum in the fifties sometimes did. A troop train was intercepted in the Brennero on the basis of intelligence his unit had gleaned. Ground attack P38 Lightnings will have seen it off. But where did we get the idea he felt those deaths on his head still now? Our dad had never fired a shot in anger. The only corpse he ever saw was after the Armistice, and his only encounter with the enemy was there in the north of Italy just after the fighting stopped, a very pleasant chap, he said, relieved to be alive and on his way back to a flattened German city beyond the Elbe.

Then came Palestine. Dad was sent there as part of the British forces supposedly policing the mandated territories, keeping the peace between Palestinians and Israelis, as they would soon become. But in fact his unit was intercepting radio signals between ships of the Russian Black Sea fleet; the Cold War already begun. And M was in the Middle East at the same time too.

Dad had been in Palestine for almost twelve months after the end of the war in Europe. Along with all the others in his unit, he'd impatiently waited for demobilization. Then, finally, in May 1946 his longed-for journey home began, travelling by train from Tel-Aviv to Alexandria, then by sea to Marseilles. After a week's wait there, they had a twelve-hour journey in a primitive train with wooden seats and nothing else. All along the railway line they found military camps where German prisoners of war were at work. In some of them the ex-Wehrmacht were well fed and in good health, but in others they too were like skeletons, something, Dad said, he would never forget. And how happy they were to reach Calais and cross the Channel to Dover. The grass in England was just so green. It was raining cats and dogs, and peace was all before them.

'What did you do in the war, Dad?' Mike and I would ask the time-honoured question, little boys in the 1950s, the whole country still getting over those years of rationing and fear. Then we'd listen with fascination and pride to this life unfolding just a few years before we were born.

Those old feelings had rather blown up in Mike's face one high-table dinner at, as it happened, Anthony Blunt's old college. Being one of the fellows' guests, he found himself seated beside the Master and engaged in occasional conversation. It turned out this distinguished personage had spent time in our part of the world during the war. He'd been in the navy and served on convoy escorts during the Battle of the Atlantic. Just to keep the conversation going, Mike mentioned that Dad had been in the Intelligence

Corps. The Master then asked did he know the joke about their cap badge? No, Mike didn't. So, for his benefit, the Master described the rose surrounded by a wreath, making sure the image was clear in my brother's mind's eye —

'A pansy resting on its laurels!'

On one occasion, talking with mum about not having children too early, she told me there hadn't been a choice for her.

'I had to have some,' she said, 'to prove your dad wasn't a sissy.'

That was before I'd come out, of course. Going to live in Italy had made it slightly easier, and now the family had at least got used to the idea. Yet it was curious to reflect, if true it were, that we'd been conceived so as to counteract a rumour, imagined or real. And what's more it wouldn't have proved anything, anyway! How miserable to think, if only in moments of depression, that this was the reason our mum had entered into the sacred state of motherhood.

We were not much older than Dad had been in 1939 on the day we went to M's flat in Pimlico. At the time, Mike said, he felt we'd somehow been a disappointment. But how should we have behaved? That imagined failure of our meeting was probably a result of M's aloneness. However willing, it was difficult to be an ear for talk when the people concerned and the terms of reference were very much over our heads.

M had booked a table at Beotys restaurant in St Martin's Lane and happened to mention that the last occasion he'd eaten there was with Graham Greene, the novelist. Greene might have been working on *The Human Factor* at that very moment. It had been another disappointment to M, who felt betrayed by the portrayal of his service in that book. But what had we detected of M's aloneness? He was unmarried, without children. He lived in a hidden world that traded in the semblances of discovered certitude, however much the market conditions required its workers to practise suspicion and doubt. M's conversation cast no shadow. Seen in another light, his words were like wallpaper behind which gaps had opened, where the winds of rumour gusted, shifting the wall surface ever so slightly.

M had said he'd kept an eye on Dad all through the war. Was that to reassure us? The name M used to refer to our dad had an air of travesty about it. 'Tommy', the name Grandma used, was what the boy growing up between the wars had been called. By the time Dad had become a chief librarian and family man in the post-war he was definitely 'Tom', the name Mum and his friends used. But M had known the delicate boy.

❧

It will have been at least thirty-five years after their acquaintance ended that a letter arrived at the house. It asked for news and invited Dad down to London to visit his old friend M. Dad must have been mystified, certainly intrigued, and no doubt a little suspicious. Why make contact after all that time? It was yet another mystery.

M's letter received a reply, filling in a little of the missing decades. After his months in Palestine and demob, Dad returned to his post in the library. It was around that time he met his future wife, a woman exactly six years younger, the duration of the war. Marrying the geography graduate, he had freed her from the agonies of teaching to a classroom-full of teenage girls. Mike and I had followed at nine-month intervals afterwards. And all the rest was literature ... library books, that is. Perhaps M knew it anyway. The invitation to visit him in London was accepted, and there were a number of subsequent meetings, a couple of lunches at Locketts, that sort of thing.

A first glimpse of this thread in Dad's past life came when, returning from a term at university, Mike picked up the copy of a Smiley novel from beside Dad's chair. When asked what it was like and why he was reading it, Dad said Le Carré's main character was supposed to be based on his old friend, M, the head of MI6. He spoke with unconcealed pride at having so distinguished an acquaintance. Apparently Le Carré always denied this supposed source of inspiration. But whether M was Smiley or not hardly mattered; he might as easily have been Ian Fleming's 'M'. Still, this man, so apparently nondescript, certainly attracted speculation. Though M may have been justifiably furious when his identity was leaked, didn't he use the chatter and gossip he was said to have relished as a form of deep cover?

So M had been gay all along. Dad's expressed assumption had proved correct. I could imagine Dad at nineteen getting involved in friendships with young men near his own age, in which however innocent or naive the occasions of meeting and talking about music, or theatre, the interest may have been partly driven by an element of attraction. Sometime after I finally told the family about my life in Italy, Mike mentioned that he too could recall unconsciously, or, better, half consciously, attracting such interest, only to be surprised and flustered should the feelings thus aroused in others even indirectly try to make themselves understood.

In the only biography of M, he is reported as regretting he didn't marry, the rumour about his sexuality categorically denied. Yet now the Prime Minister herself had told the House that M had admitted his sexual preferences, declaring he repeatedly lied about it in security clearance interviews. Perhaps that explained his well-known contempt for lie detectors when interrogating defectors. The Iron Lady had also assured the House that, despite the fact of his sexuality, he had never been a threat to national security. A patriot, Sir

M certainly was, crucially unlike his near contemporaries and enemies, deadly enemies even – Philby, Burgess, MacLean, Blunt, and others ... if others there were.

Mrs T had told the House that M was a practising homosexual in his youth before the war. But then there had been that incident in a pub in Northern Ireland involving, it was alleged, soliciting in the toilets – which had forced him to make this admission and ask the Prime Minister to accept his resignation. M a homosexual! Was that supposed to be breaking news? At the time of M's resignation it had been given out that health reasons were behind his second retirement. And he'd died of cancer just a short while after. That's how it was presented. M was supposed to have propositioned someone in the lavatory of a pub, and they'd reported it to the landlord. But could he have been set up? There were dark rumours in the papers that M, an MI6 man, had been asked by the Prime Minister to trespass on territory usually reserved for MI5. Could this have been what happened?

It was such a mystery why this distinguished servant of the state, this spymaster, had wanted to have lunch with us. At his flat we were shown those holiday snaps from the shores of the Middle East. His friends must have been his contacts. He just gave the impression of spending time with friends all round the world.

'Heaven knows what he and his friends were actually up to!' Mike had said.

At Beotys M was familiar with all the waiters, and treated them as if they were part of his staff. Back then we'd never seen anyone so relaxed with a menu. Like a Mafia godfather, he seated himself with his back to the wall. It must have been force of habit, for he did the same at Locketts, M's regular haunt in Marsham Street that was bombed a year or two later.

'That meeting with M was unreal,' Mike said, letting the paper slide off his lap onto the carpet. 'We never knew a thing about his motives.'

I had read somewhere a description of the head of MI6 as 'a lonely man with a taste for gossip over well-cooked meals' or something of that sort. Yes, we must have been a disappointment, or a sadness in some way. That was what I felt after we were dropped off at the Tate. Mike and I wandered rather dazed around the rooms of famous pictures, those representations bereft of their illusionism after our mysteriously trivial lunch. Perhaps he needed to meet ordinary people from time to time just to retain his sense of proportion.

'Or maybe he hoped to catch a glimpse of his lost youth,' Mike said, 'of Dad as he'd been back then?'

Back then, Dad had dark brown hair, sallow skin, a small nose someone once described as roman. M would also have been able to observe a life that had developed in ordinary time and space, the everyday world he saw himself and his service as protecting. He could catch up with some of the lives he believed his vocation had made possible.

Being chauffeured with M to the restaurant, we were driven past that great cottaging spot, the statue of Edith Cavell. There was one of those street artists rapidly sketching at the foot of its plinth. She was doing the double portrait of a young tourist couple. On the faced stone it gives the exact date and time of Cavell's execution, and, below it: 'Patriotism is not enough. I must hate no one.' With that statement and the example of her death, Nurse Cavell had seemed raised above questions of state. She had seemed to see the values of humanity as higher than those of a country's interests. Her bravery too was a reason for M's loneliness. The 'values of humanity': that's an empty phrase, but when demonstrated by the witness of a human life, it's given a bit more substance. In this world such demonstrations of value are perhaps less rare than we're prone to assume. As a quality that provides the motive for an action, it is usually cherished, when found – but found, because of its rarity, to exist in an ultimate, an ultimate state such as the moment of a sacrificial death. People don't inhabit such states most of the time, merely benefiting, or suffering, from the promotion of their state's perceived interests. Some, and M was one, served that interest and the interests of other nations specially allied to it.

Could a state's interests coincide with the values of humanity at large? If M had ever needed to defend his intelligence in front of some Commons select committee, if he'd had to speak up for the value of his research even though he couldn't reference it to protect his sources, if, a cradle Anglican and a practising one, he had ever sensed that the interests he served were not coincident with his higher moral values, surely he would have felt lonely? One of his tasks in life was to persuade others to betray their state's or their cause's interests. Hadn't the Prime Minister called him out of retirement to set up the super-grass system in Ulster? How had he persuaded others to betray what would have seemed to be their upheld, sustaining values when he himself appeared to be someone incorruptible?

So why then were we born English? Following rapidly upon the heels of anxieties about identity framed in terms that assume a mother country, a father land, a homeland, and unquestionably a mother tongue, came statements that implied the coincidence of the nation's interests with our own, so as to feel confident about who or what we were, a confidence which, since essentially insecure, must rest upon nothing more nor less than faith. And, as anyone who has thought or felt seriously about faith will tell you, it's groundless. Yet I too had felt with my native land, felt at one with my kind, as Tennyson put it hearing ships in the Solent gathering to depart for the Crimea, or, as we had, for the Falkland Islands, and, whatever kind that might be, being one who has also believed that the values of humanity have to be separable from those of national interest, I had also, I admit it, felt ashamed and lonely.

❧

That Sunday Mum and Dad had come over for lunch. This was why I'd taken the flight from Pisa for a weekend at Mike's. But now my big brother was in full flood.

'Didn't you see that great dent in the washing machine?' he was saying.

'No, why?' Mum asked. She was helping herself to a little more wine, Dad looking suspiciously over towards her in case she became a bit tipsy.

'I've been trying to get them to admit responsibility. The delivery men just pushed it off the back of the van.'

'I'm surprised it works at all,' said Sally.

'But would they believe me? Would they heck! They said we must have done it. So I wrote back and told them that I'd take them to court, and they wrote washing their hands, as it were, and blaming the whole thing on the delivery firm.'

'Well, it was them that did it,' said Mum.

'Of course,' said Mike, warming to his theme, 'but the manufacturers should be responsible for the behaviour of their distributors, and for the product's delivery; I mean, the satisfaction of the customer involves all of them.'

'Could I have some more carrots?' I asked, to derail the conversation. Mum passed me the plate and I helped myself.

'Anyone else want any?' I offered. 'They're delicious.'

'I had just the same problem with the paint job on my

Renault,' Mike was continuing. 'They simply could not get the colour right.'

Handing Dad the serving dish, I noticed him chuckling to himself.

'Oh yes?' he said, as if to encourage his first son to explain.

'But it was your fault in the first place, Mike,' said Sally with a frown. 'I mean you did brake far too sharply when that earthmover just juddered by the kerb. I don't think the car behind had any chance of stopping.'

'Absolutely not,' said Mike, his voice rising, 'the law states quite clearly that it is the duty of the car behind to be in a position to stop, whatever the weather conditions or state of the traffic.'

'Well, that's as maybe,' Sally returned and, turning to me, 'but the real tragedy is that he'd just that morning collected it from the showroom and, there it was, the back end with an enormous bash in it. That's where all the trouble about the paintwork came from. He just wanted to have the car brand new again.'

'Yes, all right, I admit it, but what's so wrong in that?'

'It must have been very irritating,' said Mum, 'but you'd never think anything had happened now, would you, Tom?'

Dad straightened his face just in time as the eyes of the table turned to him.

'Actually,' he said with a glint, 'I'm not sure your mother is right. If you look closely I think you can make out a faint change of tone in the metallic grey, wouldn't you say so, George?'

'Don't ask me, Dad. You know I know nothing about cars.'

Mike continued to look irritated.

'I don't believe you've even looked at the back of the car,' he was saying to Dad, and, to his wife, 'I'm sure you're right. And that's the whole point of getting them to do the job properly, even if it meant having the re-spray done three times.'

Perhaps he's worrying about his work, I thought, imagining that the accuracy required in experiments with microscopes and infinitesimal distortions in the surfaces of metals would inevitably aggravate my brother's obsession with perfect order and appearance.

We had finished the main course and Sally was clearing away the dishes when Mike's conversation took a yet more technical turn. He was explaining to Mum, who had asked a polite question, exactly what his latest research involved.

'The team I have working with me now is top class, and we're beginning to produce results that could be directly applicable to industry,' he was saying. 'The sensitivity of the microscopes is such that the slightest oversight can produce unreliable data, and that would, of course, be disastrous when I'm approaching a private company. So what the interfrometer does is register the precise fluctuations in the wave patterns of atomic particles under stress, and we can transfer these particle messages into visual form to report on the behaviour of metals subjected to structural fatigue, right down to the minutest divisions of millimeters. Its applications are everywhere: aviation safety, George, for one.'

As Mike continued to specify what the problems and the challenges were, I caught Mum's eye and smiled. I was concentrating on the plate of ice cream Sally had placed before me, wondering when my brother would stop. Then at that instant Dad began to laugh out loud. It was not a wry chuckle or smirk, but a loud and rising hilarity. He was wearing a light striped shirt with a broad maroon tie, his short soft neck folding slackly from the top of the collar, the tie falling roundly across his rounded stomach. As he began to laugh, under the influence of the glasses of wine and plates of food, his usually pallid neck and face began to flush pink.

Where was it coming from, this uncontrollable laughing? As it continued and turned his cheeks and forehead to an apoplectic plum-colour, Mike kept trying to explain his explanation, apparently unable to comprehend his father's attack of what seemed hysterical laughter. It was as if Dad were about to burst a blood vessel or suffer a massive heart attack or choke on his food – I didn't know what. He had turned such an odd bright colour. I pictured the local paper's headline: 'Father Dies Laughing at his Son's Profession'. The most glorious of glorious deaths, someone had said, to die laughing like Sir Thomas More.

Then just as suddenly the laughter died down to a purple gasping for breath, and Mike had merely to endue the chagrin of Dad's reason for this momentarily strange behaviour, once he'd recovered himself enough to explain.

'But I don't see what's so funny,' Mike couldn't help saying – which only seemed about to start another attack of the giggles from Dad.

'Really, I don't see what's so funny.'

Language Schooling

It didn't bear thinking about. He would have to get through it nonetheless. So were the Russians coming or not? The school had arranged two weeks of classes, with study visits to Stratford and London. After their acclimatization course, the twenty-four student teachers with their two leaders would divide and go to training colleges in different parts of England and Wales. It was an annual occurrence, arranged in conjunction with the British Council. But were the Russians coming this year? Were they coming or not?

Peter had done little of this type of work before. It seems you only begin to know your native language when obliged to teach it. Coming to the end of a General English course that Easter, the first he'd ever taught, Peter's nerves were fairly in shreds. Besides, out of school, he was engaged in a war of attrition with the retired brigadier who lived next door. The dispute had arisen over the old soldier's ancient lights and Peter's planning permission to rebuild his bathroom. Good fences make good neighbours. Peter had ended up with a black eye and his photograph in the *Evening News*.

In the staffroom on that last day of the Easter course, Ed Robbins, the school principal, asked Peter if he would be willing to take on the Russians.

'What would that involve?'

'Oh, hand to hand fighting, mainly,' Ed returned. 'I'm sure you'll cope well enough. Not to worry, Rod's in charge of strategy and tactics. He'll put you through your basic training – nothing to worry about – you'll do it? Fine.'

Solipsism and Self-knowledge: that was the submitted title of Peter's doctoral dissertation. It was also the year he'd been trying to draft an early chapter called 'Must We Know What We Do?' He was expected to complete by the end of September, but had run out of grant money and was running out of time. With Sylvie and baby Anna to support, living on what part-time teaching he could find, he'd put the thesis on hold to concentrate on their survival. So, naturally, when Ed offered a few more weeks' work, Peter said, 'Yes, of course, I'd love to teach the Russians a thing or two.'

Peter's mother's maiden name was, after all, Belinsky, and as Marina Belinsky she'd enjoyed a distinguished career as an actress on the London stage: little wonder, then, that she had kept her maiden name after marrying Anthony Smith, an engineer by profession. Peter, named, as he liked to imagine, after the victor of Poltawa, had been reminded all through childhood that his family's claim to compensation for property lost at the time of the Russian Revolution was still outstanding with the Soviet Authorities. Marina Belinsky had been left a widow when Peter was entering sixth form. As her only son, he felt himself heir to that claim, and, naturally enough, when their baby daughter had come along, Sylvie had accepted the inevitable and bowed to christening her child with a name that would make her husband's ailing mother happy. Yes, Peter had his reasons for wanting to teach the Russians a thing or two.

A letter arrived from the school a few days later confirming Ed's offer. It invited Peter to the first briefing session with Rod Moody.

Rod had spent years as a petty officer in the Royal Navy and was a good organizer. Stocky, with curly brown hair, greying around his ears, and lines on a forehead that was firming into middle age, Rod seemed unable to prevent himself ogling the pretty students and younger women teachers alike. What was worse, his innuendos all seemed for Peter's benefit, for the male camaraderie. Prudishly dismayed, he would be left with nothing to say. From the unease of those silences, Peter imagined Rod didn't trust him, just thought him trouble, or stuck-up perhaps.

'I've got your number,' said Rod one day, slapping Peter on the backside as he went striding by.

❧

The school's Director of Studies was required to offer literature lectures and seminars to the Russians. That was why, like it or not, he needed to get along with what, in Peter's hearing, Rod described as 'pointy-headed intellectuals'. And so it was that on a blustery morning in mid-April, Peter sat watching the branches sway between their staffroom and the office windows opposite. The trees were breaking into leaf. Loud birds were making themselves understood above the muted traffic noise. Rod and his two charges began by furnishing themselves with plastic cups of the school's poisonous coffee – used by harassed teachers to top up their nerves between lessons. There were a few unbroken biscuits left in the tin. This meeting had been timed to fall between breaks; the staffroom was empty but for the Director of Studies, Linda Wright, and Peter himself.

'Linda has agreed to take on the bulk of the specialist language teaching,' Rod explained for Peter's benefit, then, shifting his eyes to the pair-teacher: 'Actually, I had to wrestle her for it, but you won, didn't you, Linda?'

Linda nodded, indulging him, but Rod had already swivelled his eyes away.

'Pete, here, will cover the literature slots. They're doing *Romeo and Juliet* at Stratford, very popular with the Ruskies I'm told. You've heard of it, I expect. Give us a lecture on the plot, and another on the theatre in Shakespoke's heyday. You know the drill, the Globe and all that. There's a good lad. Oh, and by the way, we've decided we're going to pay you.'

Peter smiled. Linda did too. She was a solid person, plump and broad. Linda had taken the Berlitz course, got the qualification, and from her calm demeanour must have done plenty of classroom time too. The pair-teachers exchanged friendly looks. Theirs would be a two-week working acquaintance, and each knew it instantly. Since Rod had organized the course to the last detail, they had little reason to do more than exchange impressions of the students and the weather. But Peter later discovered from Rod, as if from within the services and with a peculiar awe, that Linda was actually a police sergeant's wife.

'Here are the lesson plans I've typed up for you,' Rod was saying. 'As you can see, the teacher-training sessions have been organized for the afternoons with the permanent staff. We'll be doing General English for the first period in the morning, covering the four skills, but concentrating on speaking and listening; then, after the break, we'll have two forty-five-minute sessions when you exchanges classes. I've worked in some lab slots and activities where you can bring the two classes together.'

'What will the levels be like?' Linda asked.

'The students vary from upper intermediate to advanced, sometimes practically fluent. You might have some problems with the leaders though ...'

Rod paused a moment and was duly asked why the leaders might prove difficult.

'Because it's the trusted old Party members who get to come on these visits to the wicked West – by way of a reward. Their only job is to keep an eye on the students, make sure no one defects or anything like that; but they aren't going to become teachers and don't have to know much of the language. They only follow the lessons to monitor them – make sure you're not corrupting Soviet youth with your pop music lyrics and that ... and you sometimes find the students turn out to be embarrassed by their leaders too. That said,' Rod added with one of his characteristic qualifications, 'a few of the leaders we've had coming over have turned out to be quite nice people.'

The pair-teachers had already started glancing over the timetables and lesson plans when Rod brought the meeting to a close.

'A couple of words of advice before we look at the materials,' he said. 'Among the students, there's always one male and one female Party member. They can be nuisances. You must try not to let them lead and dominate the classroom discussion. They'll probably try to monopolize the answering; you mustn't let it happen.'

'How do we do that?' Peter asked.

'Oh I'm sure you'll think of something,' said Rod, helpfully. 'It'll be interesting to see how quickly you can spot them.'

'No politics, I assume,' said Linda – merely reinforcing, perhaps for Peter's benefit, what would obviously be the case.

'Absolutely not,' said Rod, 'and especially not now. We're still not one hundred-per-cent sure they're coming, and whether the school should accept them for that matter. We thought the invasion might mean cancellation this year, what with the sanctions and all, but the regular visit was sorted out too early to be affected, apparently, and the school has reluctantly agreed to continue with the exchange programme – for this year, anyway. But the temperature has definitely dropped. There could well be difficulties, so all I can recommend is caution. We don't want an international incident now, do we, Pete.'

'Do you actually think there might be defections?' Peter asked.

'I doubt it,' the Director of Studies returned in all

seriousness. 'Remember, we're dealing with privileged people – the elite. They wouldn't be letting them out if they weren't. They'll be the children of KGB men, or that sort of thing.'

'Oh,' said Peter, his attempt at humour crushed.

'And one last thing: don't, whatever you do, and however chilly it happens to be, forget to' open the classroom windows at the end of each lesson!'

'Why so?' asked Linda.

'Because, you won't believe it; but Russians smell something awful. I don't know why, but they do, and after an hour you'll find the air's actually unbreathable ... unbearable.'

The young pair-teachers must have appeared incredulous.

'Look, I'm telling you,' said Rod, 'they really stink.'

Amongst the staffroom's piled class-sets of text books, the teachers' bags and folders, the magazines, bagged tape-recorders, stray photocopies, and other general clutter, Peter sat struggling to keep the chopped egg and mayonnaise inside the bread roll he was biting into – with just twenty minutes left in his first lunch hour.

'So far so good?' asked Peter between mouthfuls.

'That woman, the old leader,' Linda frowned, 'she's driving me spare with her totally irrelevant questions, breaking up my lesson. It's so exasperating!'

'You mustn't let her,' Rod joined in from the far side of the room, 'mustn't let them damage your authority.'

'It's not easy to get them talking, is it?' Peter put in, under his breath, for Linda's ears only. 'Did they ask you about the cheapest shops for buying clothes and presents? They did me. A bit embarrassing ... I gave them directions to Woolworth's and the British Home Stores.'

'You know their allowance of currency is severely restricted,' Rod wanted to explain. Now he was speaking from behind his staffroom desk, where, as often in the lunch break, he was signing study visit forms, company reports, teachers' pay claims, and generally making sure things were running smoothly. 'I hope you've left the windows open!'

'Yes,' said Linda, 'you were right.'

'Still not washing?' quipped Beryl, a permanent teacher who had evidently encountered the Russians on a previous visit.

'It might be something to do with their diet,' said Linda.

'Perhaps you could direct them to the nearest Boots the Chemists – oh, and give them a lesson on what the word "deodorant" means ...'

It was Ed's voice. The Principal had entered his staffroom while they were chatting, and had sat himself down opposite Rod, among the permanent teachers. It was his habit to spend a little time with them during their breaks; a means, as he saw it, for keeping in touch with their moods – moods, however, that would change the moment he entered the room.

Ed was a suave man, the son of a bishop, or so it was rumoured, well turned out in an Italian suit, a college tie, and French casual shoes. Still in early middle age, his rise from being one of the teachers in Raymond Greenwood's language school to its Principal had been rapid, and was still recalled with irony by a few of the longer-stayers. He had become a distinguished member of the local community, and Justice of the Peace, to boot.

But in his staffroom he had an unfortunate way of reminding the teachers that it was he who hired and fired. He was, thus, one of *them*; opposed, by definition, to the interests of *us*. That's how Phil, the union rep, saw it – and Phil would maintain a wary distance. Thus it was that Ed's attempts to keep a paternal eye on the school's employees had the effect of increasing his isolation, stifling, at the same time, the faltering staffroom bonhomie.

That morning's papers were, as usual, strewn about the chairs and tables. Two pieces of news dominated the front pages. The SAS had freed the hostages from the Iranian Embassy. Blurry, close-up photos of masked soldiers attacking through the building's upstairs windows appeared in most editions. We had shown, the headlines said, those Americans how to do it. A number of commentators mentioned the rescue-mission fiasco that had helped Jimmy Carter lose his presidency. Our Prime Minister had made her forceful statement about the need for a concerted opposition to international terrorism. The build-up of Soviet troops in Afghanistan was continuing to figure widely. Helicopter gunships were attacking villages, policing the suburbs of Kabul, children being maimed by antipersonnel devices. International condemnation of the USSR was threatening the success of the Olympic Games to be held in Moscow that year.

'Did you see the news last night? Rocket attacks on defenceless civilians from the air – absolutely nauseating ...' Raymond Greenwood himself had come into the staffroom, a rare event indeed. He was waving a copy of *The Times*. Rod put aside his large pile of forms and papers.

'So: how are they?' Raymond was asking.

'Jozef Goncharov's here again, his usual gentlemanly self,' said Rod, 'but there's a woman Party member who's a right pain in the bum – isn't she, Linda – who we could well do without!'

'Did you know Jozef was a war hero ... from the last war?' Ed said, rejoining the conversation. 'You know, I can't hold it against them personally, what's happening, I mean ...'

'Well,' interrupted Raymond, 'we went along with the

British Council's request that we stick to the arrangements, for this year at least, but I'm damned if that means I have to speak to any of them, even Jozef, nice enough though he may be.'

'They've asked if they can hold a party next week,' said Rod. 'Their visit coincides with the Russian public holiday to celebrate victory in the war. They want to have the day off from lessons, and a party in the common room. I've said "yes" provisionally, but told them that I would have to check with you first.'

'I think we should say that the classes have been organized and prepared, so that the students are required to attend them, holiday or no holiday,' Ed proposed. 'And you can tell them too it's not a holiday here.'

'Then if they want a party, it will have to be held after school, which seems only right,' Rod was thinking out loud.

'I suggest you put that to Goncharov,' said Raymond Greenwood decisively.

❧

Peter started up sweating from the bed with such a jump he found himself all but sitting, the sheets in a tangle around him. Sylvie lay half uncovered and snoring faintly in the pre-dawn light. Their bedroom wall opposite, with its massive poster of Palladian villas around Vicenza, had come back into focus; Peter saw where he was, and leaned over to rearrange the bed covers so that Sylvie wouldn't feel chilly and wake. His wife's nights were disturbed enough as it was. Baby Anna had already called her once with the collywobbles, but clearly she had managed to get her back to sleep. Peter lay down again, closed his eyes, and tried to doze. He had just been dreaming. Yes, thank goodness, it was only a dream.

They'd all been there surrounding him: Tanya, Alexei,

Yuri, Olga, Evgeny, Yulia, Vadim, Maria Androvna, Katya, Tatyana, Volodya, Marina, Peotr, Jozef Goncharova ... all of them. Peter was trying to pass out the pile of papers in his hands, photocopies of a poem he knew, but the papers kept sticking together, and their sharp edges cut the skin on the tips of his fingers.

'We will make a recording of every word you say,' said Alexei, in his black leather jacket, unravelling a microphone cord. 'Then we will study carefully what you have said, privately.'

'It is for the improvement of the pronunciation,' Maria Androvna said, pushing her leathery old face close up to his.

'It will be used to improve ... or, better, we'll use it ...' Peter was correcting her English in the dream.

'And we will take your photograph,' said Yuri, 'for our memories.'

Then the tape recorder began to turn inexorably on the desk.

'Say something now,' said Alexei, as if to check his recording levels.

'One must be keeping your pecker up. I can say this?' asked Maria Androvna, misreading from her Russian textbook.

'No,' said the sleeping teacher. 'No, you can't.'

'But it is here written in my book,' she said, and pushed it into Peter's face. 'Look!'

The dreaming teacher was lost for words. All twenty-eight eyes in the classroom were trained on him, as if at a firing squad.

'I'm in the red. You say this? What does it mean?'

'It means I have no money in the bank,' Peter found himself explaining. He knew just what it meant. 'In the black, you know – it's the opposite.'

'Tell me, it is Fascist in your language to have money in

the bank?' asked Jozef Goncharov, the war hero.

'Up the Reds,' said Alexei. 'You say this in Manchester?'

'Football … it's a football chant,' said the dreaming teacher.

'A red-letter day: why do you say this too?' asked Katya.

'Caught red-handed?' asked Maria Androvna. 'Why are the criminal's hands red in this one of your English idioms?'

The lying teacher didn't know.

'What is the red hand of Ulster? Do you know that?' asked Yuri.

'Please look at the piece of paper with the poem on it, will you?'

The photocopy showed three verses by Philip Larkin, the librarian in Hull.

'You will read it now,' said Alexei, turning up the volume on his tape recorder.

'Explain yourself,' said Maria Androvna. 'What is this "Oval and Villa Park"? "An August Bank Holiday lark"? Why does your Larkin talk about this bird? And this "twist"? It is the popular dance? This so-called poet of yours has spelled the word "Domesday" wrong, I see. "D-o-o-m" is right, no?'

'That's the spelling of the *Domesday Book* made by William the Conqueror in 1086. He had subjected the entire country by that date and had the book compiled to document what his conquest included; but, if you look at the words "shadowing" and "lines", there's a suggestion of the trenches in the French fields, of the shadow of death, and Doomsday, Armageddon, the end of the world, well, the end of that world anyway … It's what the poem's about, don't you see?'

But now there was that silence, the fourteen pairs of staring eyes, and tape recorder running.

'You find the poem difficult? What would you say about

the idea of innocence expressed at the end? "Never such innocence again", the poet says; what do you think he means by that?'

Still silence, no answering voice, just the fourteen pairs of staring eyes, and tape recorder running ...

'I mean it's a nostalgic poem. I'm not sure if its description of England before the Great War, yes, and the October revolution, is accurate, more tinged with a later nostalgia, perhaps.'

Deadly dead silence, the staring eyes, and tape recorder running ...

'Well, do you all know what "nostalgia" means?' said the teacher in his sleep.

Yet more chilling silence, with Peter's cheeks on fire.

'Nostalgia ... is a disease of the soul,' said Alexei from behind the tape recorder.

'Yes, interesting, a disease of the soul, that's right. It's from Greek, isn't it, and before that German, *heimweh*, because "nostalgia" was invented by a Swiss doctor to describe the condition suffered by his countrymen who were mercenaries abroad ...'

'Your poet, he is looking backward, because he cannot face the future,' said Katya. 'He is suffering from this disease of the soul ... and you ...'

'We have our own great poet of the soul, the Russian soul: his name is Yesenin,' said Maria Androvna. 'You have not heard of him?'

'I have, yes,' said Peter in his own defence. 'Sergei Yesenin. Didn't he have an affair with the American dancer Isadora Duncan? Am I right in thinking he committed suicide? Or was that Mayakovsky?'

'It was both,' said Jozef. 'Counter-revolutionaries ...'

'This man knows nothing,' said Alexei. 'He is useless to

us. Get rid of him.'

Two of the students in leather jackets had taken hold of Peter; they were lifting him backwards out of his chair; they were dragging him out of the classroom – at which point he had started up sweating from the bed with such a jump he found himself all but sitting, the sheets in a tangle around him, Sylvie half uncovered and snoring faintly in the pre-dawn light ...

❧

Yuri was pouring neat vodka into the plastic cups arranged on a row of low tables in the school's common room.

'You drink fast, like this ...'

'... in one,' said Peter and copied him – then immediately ate a biscuit with pink fish eggs to relieve the burning. Yuri was one of the two student Party members. Peter had spotted him on the second day when, by chance, they met on the stairs leading up to the classrooms.

'What did you do last night?' asked Peter, playing at being the friendly teacher.

'Nothing.'

'Didn't you go out?'

'No.'

'Did you watch television?'

At this, Yuri simply shook his head to indicate that the interview was over, turned, and strode away.

Yet now he was offering Peter another drink. Standing or sitting in clumps around the common room were all the Russians, some of the permanent staff who had taught them, Phil the union rep included, as well as Rod, Linda, and even Ed. A piano had been found and moved into one corner. The vast array of party snacks, vodka, and Georgian wine appeared care of Maria Androvna and the girl students. Yanna, the Russian Literature professor from the university, had also been invited, and a local representative of the British Council.

It was the ninth of May, and they were gathered to celebrate victory in the European theatre just thirty-five years before. Tanya and Katya were standing at the piano, while Volodya, who lived in a technology town somewhere outside Kiev, accompanied them in their singing with great gusto. Others around the room would clap enthusiastically and join in snatches. By the time he'd drunk his third neat vodka Peter was becoming seriously inebriated. Ed was deep in conversation with Jozef. Yanna smiled and joined in on the folksongs she knew in her pleasant contralto. Rod and the other members of the permanent staff were fraternizing with professional skill.

Alexei came over to Linda, who was sitting now on Peter's left. There were smiles all round and they drank a little more. Another vodka was offered, which Peter accepted and, imitating the style as best he could, downed in one.

'In the Soviet Union we make very good parties,' said Alexei.

'Yes,' said Peter quizzically, 'but can you always get the provisions ... the food? I mean we keep hearing about how you have to queue for everything and that meat is impossible to find at any price.'

'This is not true,' he said, quite categorically. 'My family eats meat every week. These reports are false.'

And as if to make his point, Alexei offered the pair-teachers another choice from the plate of cakes and sweets nearby.

Maria Androvna, meanwhile, had moved over to the piano, and, standing between Tanya and Katya, loudly clapped her hands to call for attention.

'Now we remember why we have this party,' she

announced. 'Volodya plays the pianoforte with so much genius and she accompanies the students in a song led by Katya. Katya, speak now.'

Katya took a step forward, at which all the students and leaders rose to their feet. The English teachers, faintly nonplussed, divided into those who stood up and those who remained in their seats. Yanna had come over and sat down beside Peter now that Alexei had joined the others. As they all rose, she stayed firmly seated, and Peter took his cue from her.

'Let us raise our glasses to our leader on this visit to Great Britain, Jozef Goncharov.'

Katya was speaking with a voice of authority that Peter hadn't heard before. So she must be the other Party member!

'He fought and struggled and suffered for us in the Great Patriotic War. Nor let us forget all of his comrades, heroes of our homeland who were killed by the enemy in the glorious defence of our mother earth against the invading Nazi-Fascist armies.'

A toast was drunk, which Jozef silently acknowledged. Then without further ado the whole group launched into a song. It sounded like a national anthem. Yanna remained absolutely silent. Peter leant over and asked in a whisper what the words meant.

'Oh, you know,' she answered with a smile, 'it says their country is inviolable, their armies invincible – that sort of thing.'

To the evident relief of the English sitting or standing around, the anthem came to a crescendo-ing end. Volodya immediately looked to her fellow students and struck up the buoyant lilt of a folk-dance tune. Katya's face relaxed and she attacked a cheerful verse. While some of the male students sat down to replenish their glasses, others moved a few tables and chairs back against the walls to make room for an improvised disco.

A Dansette record player had been found from somewhere and a selection of old singles furnished for the purpose. At first the girl students danced with each other. Then Alexei rose to join them, and invited Linda to dance with him, which she competently did. Peter smiled a very flushed smile at Yanna and stayed where he was. Even Yuri had got up to join the dancing crowd.

After the third record Tanya walked over towards them.

'Peter, you must dance with me!'

Tanya had become one of the most supportive students in his class. His best literature lesson had, in fact, been organized by Rod. It was an 'information gap' exercise: the students were divided up into four equal groups and each given a quarter of Somerset Maugham's 'The Force of Circumstance'. There were sets of comprehension questions to answer, and then, when each group had finished, they would be reorganized into sets of four students, one from each group, who with the aid of their bit of the text and the answers, must tell the whole story through in their own words to each other. The teacher was simply required to move from one clutch of students to another, making sure they could answer all the questions. Peter had thought the tale might have been better chosen. The force of circumstance: a British imperial wife when brought out to live on a rubber plantation discovers that her husband has 'gone native'. But he found he had thought wrong.

'It is a very fine story,' said Tanya, one of her front teeth slightly stained. 'We have known such problems already with our men who go as workers and advisors to the Middle East and Africa.'

Dance with Tanya? Hopeless as he was, how could he refuse? Peter momentarily imagined another world, the one in which his mother's family had gone on living in their Moscow apartment, and he himself, though with a different father, attending university there; he imagined himself meeting Tanya after classes for a walk in Gorky Park. Instead, he could enjoy the freedom of his overdraft, jobbing builders in his bathroom, and Sylvie exhausted from the night feeds and their worries over baby Anna's faint heart murmur.

Tanya was dressed in the bohemian style of the late fifties and sixties, half way between a jazz club habitué and a folk-rock fan. Her hair was long and straight. She had a cheerful, broad smile, and was unselfconscious about her slightly discoloured teeth. She had lively brown eyes. Tanya danced with confidence and skill, and with moderate abandon. Peter did his unconvincing best to match her.

When the song was over, as they smiled and stood uneasily together, Katya approached them.

'Tanya is our prize pupil,' she said. 'She has been selected to work as an interpreter in Moscow. We are all very proud of her.'

'At the Olympics?' Peter echoed redundantly. 'Oh, great.'

Someone put on another record. It was to be the last, so Tanya and Peter had the last dance together.

However, before the party broke up, a series of entertainments had been planned. Two of the teachers brought out guitars and sang 'The Blackleg Miner'. Then Peter was invited forward. He stepped up to the front and fumbled in his pocket for the piece of paper there.

'I'm told you all like Byron very much,' he said, 'so I'm going to read: "We'll go no more a-roving".'

'... For the sword wears out its sheath,' he read. 'And the soul wears out the breast, / And the heart must pause to breathe, / And love itself have rest ...'

Generous applause as he reached the end of the following

verse; then the students sang a last Ukrainian folk song.

There would be a final item on the programme. By special request, Phil was called upon to tell one of his jokes. He must have tried some in the classroom, because the idea was greeted with great applause.

'This is a Polish joke,' he began. 'There was this young English widow ...'

And he looked around the room with a leering smile.

'... and this English widow, see, she was living near an aerodrome in Fortress Britain during the Blitz ... and stationed there was a squadron of Polish airmen. Now this young widow had lost her husband at Dunkirk and she wanted to marry again, so she thought to herself, why don't I invite some of those nice Polish pilots to dinner one night. After all, you never know ...'

This time Phil winked saucily at Tanya as he looked about among the girls to make sure his words were getting the innuendo across.

'So she sent an invitation to the aerodrome and, on the night, the squadron's colonel, a major, and a handsome young captain arrived for supper.

Anyway, everything passed off well enough. All the courses were eaten and warmly praised, the drink flowed and then, the acorn coffee served, this widow decided to find out whether the young captain was married or not. But how would she do that? I know, I'll ask him if he has any children. So, as they were all sitting back contentedly, sipping the acorn coffee, she asked: "Captain, you and your wife, do you have any children?"

"Alas, no, madam," replied the captain, "we do not have any children. My wife, you see, she is *unbearable*."

The young widow's face dropped – her plan for finding an eligible bachelor in ruins. The major could see that something was wrong with what his junior officer had said.

"Madam, please excuse my fellow officer. The captain's English is not so good. He means to say 'My wife is *inconceivable*'."

The young English widow looked no happier. So the colonel, seeing that the evening had suddenly taken a disastrous turn, decided he must rescue the situation.

"My dear lady," he said, "the English of my officers, it is far from what it ought to be. My young captain here, forgive him, madam, he means to tell you that his wife is *impregnable*'."

After so much vodka, the dancing, and the adrenalin of reading in public, Peter couldn't help it: he was laughing convulsively. So were Rod and the other permanent teachers. Ed and Jozef had smiled. Linda was looking at the floor. Yanna was staring at Phil, not laughing at all. Maria Androvna wasn't either. She hadn't got the joke. Tanya was certainly smiling. Peter could see through the tears that came rolling down his cheeks. He had pulled out a hanky and quickly pretended to be blowing his nose.

'So what is the word the Polish airman should have used?' asked Phil with his professional teacher smile.

But not one of the Russian students seemed to have any idea.

Pain Control

'... non so quel ch'io mi voglio,
e tremo a mezza state, ardendo il verno.'
Francesco Petrarca

Stood on its slope with my back to the bombed-out shell of St Luke's Church, kept up at some expense – as Patrick said – for a Blitz memorial, I was gazing down Bold Street towards the Pier Head. It was my first visit to the city made famous by *Gli Scarafaggi*. Yes, that's what they're called in Italy. It was the translation of a spelling mistake: I knew they weren't called The Beetles. When I'd asked where to buy things in Liverpool, Patrick's mother gave me directions to Bold Street. And she told me that, during the city's heyday, it had been one of its most posh places to shop. And it was true you could still pick out a few remnants of the place's former glory. There was its painting materials business that served the nearby Art School, three bookshops, and a post office with classical façade. Among them now were the ethnic groceries, their rare scents reminding me of my Indian travels. There were sad-looking cafés, empty windows, boarded-up premises ... It seemed a place for the poor and left behind.

I was standing outside the Emporium, a health food store with a fancy emerald frontage that showed it had been other things before, though not being a native, what they were I couldn't quite tell. On the point of closing down, selling off the last of its stock at ridiculous prices, the Emporium still had a cardboard box full of tea tree soap. I'd jumped at the chance and bought four bars. Change slipped safely into my jeans' pocket now, I glanced at my watch. It was a little after midday, the day sweltering hot, a Friday in the middle of summer. There on Bold Street, the sunshine had me narrowing my eyes against its glare. I found my sunglasses and put my straw hat back on. It was not at all what I expected, this city, so sweltering hot up in the English North. Patrick's father, as a matter of fact, liked to call it the *Costa del Merseyside*.

But as I was standing there, half-lost in thought, a rough-looking man, his beard flecked with vomit, lunged forward and slurred a request for his bus fare home. He had grasped me firmly by the hand. I gave what I thought must be a visible shiver.

'Remember that social worker, years back, who was killed?'

Unsteady on his legs, the chap was giving off a telltale reek. I allowed his swollen pink hand with its cracked and dirty fingernails to keep possession of mine; but before I could even think of a suitable reply, the man said –

'My wife.'

'*Mi dispiace...*' I blurted out, and when he looked blank, 'I'm sorry.'

'I'm not very drunk, though, am I?' he added, with tears in his eyes and as if to repent.

I found a few coins from my pocket and pressed them into his other dirty hand.

'God bless you ... God bless you,' he said, without taking his eyes from my sun-tanned face.

'She never should have left me,' he sobbed, his hand still clinging on to mine.

Alone again on Bold Street, under the estate agents' signs with their partnership names and phone numbers, I glanced into my two large plastic shopping bags, mentally checking the list – arnica to rub on Patrick's needle bruises; a pair of blue cotton pyjamas; a new toothbrush; enough fresh fruit to fill his bowl; a Raymond Chandler omnibus;

the vitamin B tablets ... That was enough. That would surely do for now. It was time to get back to his bedside. Surrounded by the racket from road works required for its pedestrianization scheme, I could see how the fashion boutiques had given way to Oxfam and Save the Children there on old Bold Street.

❧

It was best to take a taxi. I couldn't really afford one, but the buses were just too confusing.

'Walton ... Walton General ... Hospital,' I told the driver after he wound down his window and leaned out towards me.

Now with the shopping bags on the seat beside me, I was sitting back in that cab being taken down Prescott Road towards the Old Swan, watching the blackbirds and sparrows drop down to their worm-filled ground. How oddly things had turned out!

We had met first in my hometown, where Patrick would come on business trips for an import–export firm. Looking back on those first meetings, it seemed clear enough something of the sort was bound to happen. Though he'd never made a secret of being married, Patrick had become infatuated. At the time, I admit, I enjoyed his company, but didn't expect it to go anywhere – and yet I should have known from that hangdog look of his, and the way he paid such attention to every last thing I would say. No, I was by no means infatuated, just flattered by his attentions – attentions that were easy enough to relish and resist. But the third time he came and pressed himself upon me that bit more firmly, I'd allowed my growing temptation to have its way. And, of course, I should have known. After all, Patrick was a married man ... and a hopeless liar. His wife Jennifer found out, as she was bound to, and my more or less literally one-time lover, the man with whom I was now in love, had tried his best to make a complete disappearance from my life.

The black cab was trundling on along broad avenues of the city, the place full of those little English houses made of brick with cared-for bits of garden at both front and back. What most surprised me about Liverpool was how green it looked. It was hardly like my idea of a seaport town in the grim industrial North. There were so many wide stretches of parkland with sycamores and beeches in full summer leaf. There were strips of grass down the sides and middles of the boulevards, ones often lined with plane trees themselves. Before coming here, I just assumed it must be a place like Genova; but the people, it was clear, were quite different from the Genoese – whose dry sense of humour could be mistaken for cynicism or spite. No, the place Liverpool most resembled was Napoli, with its accent that even I could scarcely penetrate, its traditions of song writing, and famous comic vein – traditions I imagined must have taken root here for much the same reasons.

And as that black cab rattled on, I found myself remembering what looked at the time as if it would be our final sad parting.

'*Carissimo*,' I was saying, '*mi pare che questo per te sia un vero calvario.*'

Patrick, standing there before me, looked acutely uncomfortable.

'*Carissimo*,' I repeated, and embraced him. He gave a weak smile, turned, and, without looking back, disappeared into passport control.

I had driven to Bergamo, and was waiting to ambush him there in its tiny check-in lounge: wearing my favourite full skirt, a Chinese jacket, and the shoes with a single strap fastened by a tiny button. Ever the nervous traveller, Patrick was giving himself plenty of time to catch that Stansted flight. So his anxieties about missing the plane had provided me with the best part of an hour to talk.

I've never been able to conceal my emotions. My face is their perfectly tuned instrument.

'Why didn't you come?' I asked.

'I explained in my letter,' Patrick replied.

The letter was the latest in a series of conflicting signals he'd been sending, and it was as if at the sight of me there in the airport his resolution had failed him again. He just didn't know what he wanted. He would tell me I was irresistible. He said it was the freckles across the bridge of my nose, the laughter lines about my eyes, that slight curling up of my top lip when I smiled, a smile that revealed the pink gums above my slightly gapped front teeth – something I'd worried long about in the mirror. My long ear lobes, he said, were like a patient Buddha's.

Pulling himself together, pushing back his quandaries of burning, burning and regret, he told me again there at the airport, told me the only thing he could: if he had come to see me even that once more, as he promised, there would have been too much pain to bear.

But the course of true love, as they say in English, never did run smooth – and I had found my own painful feelings at his attraction and rejection reawakened one spring morning when a postcard arrived from Patrick asking to come and see me for a day or two. He needed, the postcard said, to talk.

And it was as if my prayers on those nights of biting my pillow had miraculously been answered. Patrick's wife, a social worker as it happened, had convinced herself that after his briefest of flings with me, no matter now hard he tried, her husband would never be able to forget his foreign affair. She would never be able to forgive him for what – I had to think – had been an awfully small and short-lived lapse. So after those years of silence, here he was telling me his marriage was over and, despite the old equivocal behaviour towards me, would I be willing to give it a go?

Though I naturally treated his declarations of love with a certain caution, I really didn't need asking twice. But then, yet once more, it seemed my chance of happiness was to be snatched away – this time, by death. No sooner had we got together than Patrick started to complain of recurrent headaches. One morning he climbed out of bed, vomited, and collapsed on the floor, his hands clutching the back of his skull. At the local hospital, the doctors found something that shouldn't have been there in his brain. Patrick was given strong medicines, the kind that I was against on principle, and sent back to his city to have the operation they said was absolutely essential if his life were to be saved.

But I just had to be there when he went in for surgery. That had made it more difficult for everyone, for Patrick's parents, his estranged wife no doubt trying to lure him back, and for those friends of his I'd never met before. No I couldn't not be there, and didn't want to lose him after all we'd been through. But after his ten days in hospital for the operation itself, and then the painfully slow stages of Patrick's return to minimal functioning, the strain had begun to tell. It seemed I might still have to leave and go back home. Too many changes were happening all at once. His beautiful smile could never be the same. Patrick had started calling his wife Jenny again. Perhaps Jennifer would even get him back after all. It was just too much to bear. I kept breaking down in tears, then, as a result, feeling even more ashamed of myself.

I thought of the adopted stray cat sunning itself on Patrick's parents' concrete patio, the warm light tinting their garden, emphatic on the damp wood fencing beyond an emerald green lawn speckled with daisies. The convalescent day's empty ease was unravelling on the flowerbeds where a broken branch had settled. It lay cushioned on the clump of nettles I'd promised to cut down. I was going to make some soup of them. Patrick's father was a retired psychotherapist ... and as his mysteriously bad-tempered comments crashed over his mother and me like breaking waves, I could do nothing but stare, once more on the verge of tears, at a bowl of rose petals imperceptibly aging on the parlour window ledge.

At the moment of his relapse, Patrick's precarious day had contracted to a worsening headache's dual hells of shivering fever, sweaty chills, and nothing else at all. In fact, the local doctor didn't know what it was. It could be meningitis, he said. Better be on the safe side, he said. Because they happened to have a spare bed, Patrick was admitted to the Pain Control Unit, put on intravenous penicillin, the butterfly valves taped to his wrists. That would knock those symptoms on the head, they said. Not that it was meningitis, they eventually discovered, but an inner ear infection tracking back towards the site of his operation – the wounds hardly healed and leaving behind all kinds of collateral damage. At night a sticky liquid would ooze from his right ear to stain the pillowcase with horrid dried-blood-coloured spots.

As my darling lay there with that burning head, that suspected meningitis, asleep under the morphine, I would sit silent by his bed. I had never had occasion to spend such time in a hospital before, and certainly not an English one where they didn't even let family members come and look after their loved ones. Each morning, the men would relate their histories of the night. Arrived early, I would be watching a magpie peck at the mossy concrete on the rooftop of the Outpatients Department opposite. Beyond it, there lay an urban skyline of neat brick gables, a fly-over and tall church spire.

'Pain is pain: it wears you down,' said the Royal Airforce Band cornet player from his sedated sphere, 'like water running over a stone.'

'Oh shut the fuck up,' murmured Alex, but loud enough to be heard.

Alex was sitting in his bed, the pillows piled behind him, a sheet pulled over his legs, and that morning's opened *Mirror* laid across them. He must have been about forty, and had been in pain for twenty years. He was from Belfast, where he'd caught a stray bullet meant to kill a soldier. Once, while he was being bed-washed by the nurses, I saw the scar tissue of its entry and exit wounds. The bullet had grazed his spinal cord, and, despite the so many operations he'd lost count, Alex remained paralyzed and in pain.

'Papish bastards,' I heard him mutter one day as he read his paper, and made a mental note to keep my silver crucifix and rosary well out of sight.

Alex had tried everything to ease his suffering. Booze was the mainstay for years. Neat gin or vodka worked the best, he said. But then he found he was in effect an alcoholic too and had to go to the meetings to wean himself off the demon drink. He'd even experimented with banned substances, but the side effects were so much worse. What really saved his life in the end, he said, was finding that, notwithstanding the state he was in, one of the young women from social services was offering to marry him. That's how I found out he had a wife and kids back home in Ireland. Alex was keen to get his slow drug-release implant fixed so he could return to the life that, in spite of everything, fate had allowed him to make.

It was only a day or two later – Patrick off the morphine – that Alex began a two-week acquaintance with my boyfriend by giving him a wink and a flattering glance in my direction.

'Well,' he said, now *'you're* a lucky man!'

❧

'You could spend your holidays here!' somebody chuckled beside me.

I had paid the taxi driver and, laden with the plastic bags of shopping, pushed my way through the sprung doors into hospital reception. All around were the shaved heads and bandaged limbs of patients – some pushing their IV supports round on wheels with the drip needles still in their arms. I headed towards the corridor that led round to the lifts for the various wards. There was a continuous flow of traffic going by as I walked: unsteady feet, stretchers, wheelchairs, doctors with the white tails of their coats blowing up behind them, and the visitors, finding their way, looking faintly embarrassed to be in the best of health.

During the two weeks that Patrick was up on the ward, I came to appreciate how the Liverpudlians who worked there managed the routines of pain and its control. Each morning one of the orderlies would write on a whiteboard 'The Daily Joke'. Though I had to admit my English was not good enough to understand them, I did think it such a lovely idea. Patrick told me about how the night nurses would give him a cocktail of two pain-killers, not supposed to be used at the same time, but which when taken together helped you get a good night's sleep. That Saturday evening, since to all intents and purposes there was nothing wrong with him, some of the nurses were planning to spirit Alex out of the ward for an evening in the pub down the road ...

The lift up to the Pain Control Unit was empty for once.

As it juddered to a halt and the doors opened, I grasped my two plastic shopping bags and, stepping forward, found myself engulfed in a great crowd of people. They had been silent as the lift doors opened, but now were laughing loudly and smiling at each other. What was going on? There were three camera crews, some photographers with flashguns, and journalists holding microphones towards me. Stationed in amongst them were the wheelchairs and stretchers of immobile patients – with their eyes all trained upon me. Some of the walking wounded had positioned themselves strategically craning their necks just to catch a glimpse of me. Among them were the faces of nurses and even some junior doctors I had come to know during Patrick's stay on the ward. Momentarily bewildered, I looked around for the bandaged head of my nearly fatally damaged young man.

Patrick was standing at the far end of the corridor, as distant from the lift as he could get, with Alex beside him in his chair. Alex was clearly doubled up in stitches. Patrick had a hand over his half-paralyzed mouth. He seemed to be laughing too, laughing till it hurt. But I had no idea what was supposed to be so funny.

❦

So then they told me how, that very day, Her Royal Highness, the one with the freckles and russet curls, would visit the unfortunates who fell within the scope of her charity's care. That was why the orderlies, the nurses, the news people, walking wounded, those on trolleys and in chairs had been waiting in a hush of expectation near the lift.

Then suddenly, just as the boys were explaining, Her Royal Highness came sweeping out of the lift with her entourage around her. Mingling with the gathered crowd, she stooped slightly forward, turning her head just a little to one side.

'And how have you been keeping?' she asked an old lady who could hardly contain her excitement at being addressed by celebrity.

'Yes, indeed, it's your health matters most,' Her Royal Highness was saying to another.

But now Patrick and Alex were taking cover in the side ward. While my wounded love climbed back under the sheets, I took the liberty of drawing the curtains around his bed. Then I perched myself on the coverlet beside him. And at that moment it seemed more than likely that this being mistaken for somebody else was how he would remember me – the embodiment, he'd told me, of his second chance at happiness. That hubbub of excitement dropping down to a hush at what was supposed to be Her Royal Highness's lift arriving, its doors slowly opening to reveal ... only an upset for boom-mike and camera, no glad-handing princess, a cliché on her lips. No, but there, momentarily astonished, with full plastic bags beneath the world's eye and smiling, smiling the smile that showed the gums above my slightly gapped front teeth, only me, my flesh and blood and bones, a bewildered self in that foreign land alone.

National Lottery

'So let me see now ... "At the time of your first marriage, where did you plan to be buried?"'

The Consul looked up. His pen hovered over the form with its column of questions. He had warned you some were unusual. The Consul's pate glistened through his bar-code haircut. He wore a precisely trimmed moustache, and carried the *embonpoint* of a man who enjoys his food. The Consul had evidently spent much of his life abroad. He displayed the graceful condescension of one who knew his station, one become accustomed to the experience of others knowing theirs around him. Yet was there a trace of some obscure province in his almost accentless Received Pronunciation? If so, it was long dead and buried. So, now, where were we? Here's where you were: in the Consul's office, sitting before him, silent and staring – as if he were the one with the attitude problem. The Consul offered a slight, a would-be apologetic smile.

Outside, the rain continued to fall, nothing of a British drizzle about it, rather the full-scale Asiatic downpour. The liquid daylight was momentarily overshadowed as an unfurled umbrella passed outside. Then it glimmered through the transparent plastic of one bought at a convenience store, somebody caught in the rain without her own. The guard on the Embassy Gate had his lodge to keep him dry. He'd nodded you through on catching the repeated, one-word purpose of visit. Like a castle armoury, crowded racks of umbrellas dripped in the Consulate's entrance.

A woman in her thirties came into the office. She dipped slightly, mumbling her apology for interrupting, and balanced a piece of paper on the edge of the Consul's desk. The secretary had muddy specks up the backs of her ankles.

It was ten past eleven on a dull day in the latter part of June. As she was leaving, the Consul asked his secretary to bring two cups of coffee, milk, and no sugar for his co-national, yes, and biscuits. With the slightest of bows, she turned and disappeared.

This interview at the Consulate, overlooked by a photographic portrait of Queen Elizabeth II in her younger days, would be the final hurdle. Truthfully answer the series of questions, and your daughter could be granted her passport without further delay. But here was the snag: when you married your first wife, you weren't even planning to die. The thought of where your expired corpse might be buried hadn't so much as crossed your mind.

'When you married your first wife ...' No, that cheerful girl in white veil and bridal gown, being photographed amid grime-smutted gravestones, hadn't even seemed your first one at the time. Barbara Penny, with her rare maiden name, used to say she'd make sure to die first. So you could be the one who pined away from grief. But would you have the face to attend her funeral now? So where did *she* plan to be buried? Barbara preferred to be cremated, she'd said, and her ashes scattered across some barren moor – and this other wife? Isabella doubtless hoped to be interred at the municipal cemetery of her birthplace, near the graves of so many dear departed.

And all because nationality comes through the mother ... that was where our problem started, or, at least, why we had one. Our only daughter hadn't, unfortunately, been born in the United Kingdom. She was brought forth alive by caesarean section five months before you were free to marry her mother. Clara might have been, speaking technically, an accident, but neither of her parents were getting any younger. She was far from the unwanted love child of fable.

No, admit it, you were just a fond, foolish old father who, sixteen months before, had still not quite reached the end of the reconciliation period in a 'no fault' divorce.

Then there had been that brought forward and re-scheduled last leg of a fourteen-hour flight so as to be at the *Ospedale Maggiore* and acknowledge little Clara before she was sent into the outside world with her first official document stamped 'father unknown'. The ceiling fan wobbled on its stem in the maternity unit as you sat at her pale and gaunt mother's bedside, allowed to hold the little mite, your daughter, with her fingers so tiny and stick-like you were afraid to touch them for fear they would come off. Yet there she was, a part of life: six weeks premature, illegitimate, though with an ex-pat Brit for a dad. By this means Clara did at least have two as yet unmarried parents, was a native of Puglia, and a citizen of the Italian Republic – on account of having been born there, and seeing as she was her mother's daughter.

The rain continued to bounce on the concrete walkway that ran beside the Consul's glass office wall. There was a hinged, double picture frame standing on top of his bookshelf. In one wing was the colour photo of a woman in oval-shaped sunglasses, with long black hair pulled tightly back from her angular features. She was posed before a conquistador-style hacienda. In the other were two olive-skinned children, a boy and a girl. Each displayed a toothy, shining grin.

The Consul picked up a transparent plastic folder crammed with the relevant documents.

'So,' he began, 'I see you failed to have your illegitimate daughter's birth registered with the British Consulate in Rome ... and that, if you'll allow me to say so, was your first mistake.'

'I didn't think there'd be a problem, me being English.'

'Ah but, as you soon found out, there was – at least one,' said the Consul, underlining the obvious.

Yes, we soon discovered our mistake. Don't even try to apply for your daughter's British passport until you're married to the mother, an old Asia-hand advised us. Nor would it be a case of walking up that well-known aisle. One of those bittersweet afternoons of confetti, feasting, and speeches was more than enough. When the Decree Absolute had come through, you telephoned the Consulate and enthusiastically inquired what we had to do to get wed, in a civil ceremony, there, at the Consulate, on what was, after all, British territory?

'I'm afraid you can't,' came a voice down the line. 'You see, unless the Consulate is in a country where the religion will not permit it, our policy is to publish the banns here in the Consulate, then inform the local government office where you are residing that we have declared you legally free to marry.'

The official will have heard a loud gasp of surprised exasperation down the phone.

'Your marriage must be performed by the local authorities and recognized as a marriage within the legal system here,' her explaining voice continued.

'But you seem to have made things difficult for everyone, don't you?' said the Consul, benignly. 'Why didn't you follow the standard procedure?'

Not being nationals of our country of residence here in Asia, and the language so notoriously difficult to master, neither of us would have understood the majority of official words uniting us – let alone been able to read our own marriage certificate. Then that scrap of paper would have had to be translated into two or three languages, at least, so it could serve its bureaucratic purpose on our pilgrimage through expatriation's vale of whatever it might be.

'As you know, my wife is Italian, and neither of us speaks much of the local language ... '

So naturally enough, you had called the Consulate of your second wife-to-be and found they would happily perform the marriage in a tongue you could more or less understand on what was technically Italian and European Community soil. So there we were, standing in front of a large polished table, surrounded by walls of almanacs and, beside them, a print of The Temple of Concord in Rome, a large parchment-like sheet laid out before us, the presiding under-secretary wearing a red, white and green sash. The long civil document was read aloud in the three differently relevant languages.

With punctilious anti-clerical zeal, the marriage document spelled out what precisely were the social purposes of matrimony, what rights were conferred and what duties required. It made a point of retroactively legitimizing Clara, and informed us that within six months, were you resident in the Republic of Italy, and within three years if not, you would yourself be entitled to apply for nationality. It was only as we left the Italian Consulate by way of its reception waiting room that we noticed and remarked on an enormous advert for the *Superenalotto* attached to its dingy off-white walls.

'That's as maybe,' said the British Consul, 'but I take it you appreciate that this stratagem of yours put us in quite a quandary. We have our protocols, to which we must adhere, all laid down in agreements signed by the British and local governments, and these do not make provision for marriages conducted on alien territory within this country. You see, my staff were perfectly correct in informing you that this Italian marriage of yours could not be recognized by the United Kingdom authorities, because the ceremony had *not* taken place on local territory and had *not* been recognized by the relevant powers that be.'

'Fog in the Channel ...' you thought yet again.

'Though I have to admit,' he went on, 'it was a clever dodge of yours to get the immigration people here to recognize this Italian marriage certificate.'

He had slipped the photocopy out of its folder and was waving it in the air, looking like nothing so much as Neville Chamberlain as he descended the steps of his plane from Munich, announcing peace in our time once more.

'What you should have done,' he continued, with a kindly paternal air, 'is simply accept the formality of a second marriage in the local ward office, not go trying to wriggle through that loop-hole.'

The Italian marriage certificate had been conveniently supplied with a translation. So we had taken it to our provincial city's overcrowded Immigration Office, filled out the bundle of forms required, purchased the document taxation stamps from the nearby post office, returned, frittered away some more time in the queue, and submitted a request for two dependent-status visas: one for a newly-wed wife and one for a legitimated daughter.

To qualify for such visas, the persons must of course re-enter the country with the correct documentation entitling them to apply, within thirty days, for dependent status. It was naturally not possible to substitute these visas for the short-term tourist-status visas while remaining in the country itself. Your new, second wife had pages of such stamps in the back of her passport. It was starting to look suspicious. More than once an immigration officer had advised her, seeing that the man accompanying her had a resident-status stamp, to apply for the correct visa.

Little did he know that it was only by Bella's and Clara's repeatedly pretending to be tourists that our little family had
managed to remain united ... while the divorce proceedings
with Barbara trudged on their wandering and solitary way.
Being aliens in a foreign land had now also obliged you to
make an honest woman out of Bella.

The Union Jack was more or less still flying on Peaks
Road as that vintage double-decker bus leaned out round its
switchback curves. Bella clung on tight to Clara as we were
scrutinized by a grey-haired administrator-type in a three-
piece suit, a fob watch, and university-blue tie. It was the
double-decker buses that had clinched the similarity; but,
even before seeing them, there was something curiously
nostalgic about the police uniforms and postboxes. Clara's
pushchair steady on the Star Ferry's planking deck, she was
borne on the waves between container ships, lighters and
junks, with the flashing glass spires of insurance offices,
merchant banks and consulates in the distance. After
only an hour on Nathan Road, her little face was flecked
with black smuts from the air. Down in the bird market
overlooked by rickety balconies on the tower blocks' drab
frontages, mynah birds, parrots and budgies competed with
the bargaining in a rapid-fire Cantonese ...

So after a couple of days in Hong Kong we were enabled
to re-enter this country having secured the correct official
documents and stamps. Thus the immigration services for
our place of residence had, effectively at least, recognized
the Italian marriage as legally furnishing me with a pair of
dependents.

'We frankly had no alternative but to contact our legal
department in London,' the Consul continued. 'I've never
had to deal with another case like it, you know, not in all my
years with the service!'

Finally and at last, back came an answer from the people

at the relevant ministry. Yes, these two European citizens, with documents that proved them to have been married on European territory, and further documents that evidenced the *de facto* recognition of this marriage by the authorities of their country of residence, could indeed be recognized by the British state as married. Which is how it came about that, after all the separate journeys, the telephone calls and paperwork involved, you were sitting before the Consul attempting to answer that series of questions.

'Since your daughter is to be granted citizenship on the basis of your own claim to United Kingdom nationality, it is necessary to authenticate these qualifications,' the Consul had explained. 'Let me just confirm ... your passport number is?' 120652B. 'Were your four grandparents born in the British Isles?' 'Were your two parents born there?' 'Do you own any property on British Crown territory?' But this time the answer was 'no, you didn't'. Your first wife, Barbara, she'd been gifted with it all as part of that 'no fault' divorce.

'So,' the Consul said, 'at the time of your first marriage, where did you plan to be buried?'

The Consul had repeated his question. But what could you possibly tell him to complete his pink official form?

'I know it's an odd one,' he candidly admitted, 'but as you'll appreciate this questionnaire is not exactly designed for cases like yours. We sometimes have to process applications from polygamous cultures and ones with very extended families. I'm sure you see what I'm getting at ...'

But answer came there none.

'... and I wonder,' he continued, 'have you had any similar difficulties – living, as you appear to do, not only here but also at least some of the time in Italy? Their red tape's notorious the world over, is it not?'

'Well, as a matter of fact, we have,' you admitted, 'but nothing quite like this!'

Unabashed, the Consul took up with his left hand the skeleton *curriculum vitae* you had sent for the purpose of proving your patriotism. He was glancing down the lists: schools, universities, degrees, precarious posts, hand-to-mouth hourly paid employment, bread-line literary jobs – not a thing you could use as supporting evidence with Barbara when rehashing the same old arguments about how it was time to start a family.

The Consul sipped at the coffee his secretary (apologizing for interrupting us) had brought in. He thanked her with his graceful condescension. The Consul glanced from the *CV* out over his desk. The coffee was still too hot to sip.

'Sorry,' you said, apologizing for the silence. 'There's no answer … I was twenty-six … I wasn't even thinking of dying.'

'Better not leave a blank,' the Consul immediately advised. 'Go on, just make something up.'

How about beneath those rugged elms, or in that yew-tree's deepening shade? Or should it be in some corner of a foreign field? And which part, precisely, of our Sceptred Isle was supposed to constitute your native ground? You can bury my body under the railway viaduct at Berwick on Tweed. Or take me back to Carrickfergus … Anywhere in the United Kingdom and Northern Ireland would surely do … but, still, you couldn't resist. He did say make something up.

'How about "in the Heart of England,"' you replied, with a smile.

'Now where would that be?' he wondered, without one. 'I'll put down Shropshire.'

'But Bunbury is exploded,' you didn't, of course, say, picturing the gravestones in Isabella's hometown cemetery, with their tiny photographic portraits of wife and husband lying beside, or on top of, one another. Yet in the quiet of his office, with a coffee cup raised to your lips, you were consenting with a nod to the Consul. You would stand by his fiction. Now that he'd written it down, 'Shropshire' was no longer a convenient invention to get out of a fix. He'd transformed it into a fact about your life.

There were still further gaps to fill out on the form.

'Where will your daughter be educated?'

You alluded to the British public school system.

'Where have you invested your money?'

You mentioned some household names in the UK financial services industry ...

And so it went on to the end.

Now, despite his occasional and momentary frowns, it seemed there was wind in our sails. You would complete the questions and, in due course, be entitled to apply in the usual fashion for a small maroon booklet that would let Clara into the Consul's country (and hers) with not so much as a wave of the hand.

But who was it said being born British meant – and still meant, despite all the blows to national pride – drawing a winning card in the lottery of life? And come to think of it, was anybody ever actually plucked from a mother's womb British? How could all those tiny, bloody, bawling babies be allowed to pass freely without let or hindrance and be afforded such assistance and protection as may be necessary in the Name of Her Majesty the Queen?

Fair enough, but you admit you were born and raised in England. If you so much as tried to pass yourself off as Scots, Welsh, or Irish, despite the family's twilight ancestry, people from those countries would quickly and firmly put you in their idea of your place. Belonging was something that other people did. Still, whatever your passport, you were English right enough. It was there in your way with consonants and vowels: no escaping that, and little you could do about it either. What's more, whoever said being born British was like winning the lottery of life had got something right at least. It was chance. A shining finger of fate would reach out of the sky and touch the daily existences of some average folk sitting around a TV screen – till each one dropped by lottery. Our number would come up ... or we would draw a blank. The probability was just the same for any series of digits every time. No question of deserving it, and no justice in it either. Winning was quite as shameless as having lost.

Yet still, we had won! At least the Consul was reaching the end of that pink official form. He had even allowed himself a certain smile.

'But should your daughter marry a foreigner, your grandchildren will have no right to become citizens of the United Kingdom,' he was explaining, visibly relaxing a little.

The Consul's eye caught you glancing over towards his family photographs up there on the bookshelf.

'This is not the case, by the by,' he went on, 'for Civil Service employees stationed overseas. Their offspring, wherever they were born and whatever the nationality of the other parent, are granted the full citizenship of children born on British soil. After all, they were only born abroad because one or both of their parents was serving the Crown.'

The Consul had risen and come round from behind his desk. You stood up to leave, and shook his hand. He reminded you to pick up the passport application form from the reception window before leaving. Finally, as an expression of his goodwill towards a fellow countryman, the Consul assured you, nodding towards your *CV* on his desk, that should you wish to return to Britain at any time, with your experience and qualifications, you would surely find suitable employment.

'But, if you don't mind me saying,' he added, 'I do think you've gone about this all the wrong way.'

From the Stacks

It will have been one of those melting days towards winter's end. I don't know why, but they're days when I can't seem to settle to anything. Perhaps it's the sun's angle at that time of year, casting long shadows over the still crisp ground, the leafless trees' branches traced like vein-work and arteries over the paths that I'm drifting along. The school year coming to an end, suddenly the old campus is overcrowded with students heading for exam rooms. Yet despite being surrounded, I still have the feeling I'm just not there at all. No, I've never been able to work out if it's because I'm an alien, or just the rigid hierarchy in which we're all inescapably located. Faculty being on another plane, it's out of the question for freshmen or sophomores to so much as acknowledge our existence, and if you even attempt to condescend to their level, they're so flustered by the collapse of order that they don't know what to say, and, to save face, will simply cut you dead.

Naturally enough, after a while, you accept this last straw, and blank them too. Well, anyway, as I say, especially at that moment of the year, to minimize the chance of such non-encounters, I'll go the other way along my corridor, out of the emergency exit and onto the iron fire-escape bolted to the end of the Arts Faculty block. Trying not to glance over the edge as I emerge and shiver in the chilly winter air, the eight-floor drop bringing on my vertigo, I'll float down the stairs where, it has been rumoured, more than one desperate undergraduate has ended it all.

Through the higgledy-piggledy chaos of students' bicycles I'll slide my way past them and on through the long shadows of branches towards the refectory and faculty-only restaurant. Often, unable to settle to anything useful, I would get up from my desk far too early for lunch and, as a last resort, take myself off to the library and hover about the shelves in its capacious basement. There's practically no chance of meeting anyone down there. Only members of the academic staff have the privilege to look at the books, and hardly anyone, it seems, takes advantage of it. There's a central stairway down to the lower floors and vast, cavernous rooms branching off to left and right. To the right are the post-1972 acquisitions, to the left the older holdings. The newer volumes have fixed, open shelves; but the dustier tomes are kept in what I can only describe as concertina stacks. Entering their room, you're confronted with a vast box-like structure, a facing wall of pale green metal shelves – but closed together, without the space between them even to browse. On each shelf there's a button in front of you that lights up when you push it, and, open-sesame-fashion, the two shelves part sufficiently to allow you to walk between them and hunt for your item. It's the only place where I've ever come across such an arrangement and, given my never having encountered a soul down there, I was obliged to discover how the system worked by trial and error. It was the way I fathomed out that it's impossible to open a second stack, which will automatically close the first, until you have turned the first light off by pressing the button again. Of course, it had crossed my mind to wonder what would happen if the system were tampered with and the stacks closed when I was in there thumbing through some long-forgotten treatise. It would be a fate like one of those in Edgar Allan Poe – a fine, century-old edition of whose *Tales of Mystery and Imagination* you'll find on the third shelf down in the first American literature stack, but mistakenly catalogued under E.

As I say, it was one of those warm days near winter's end, the sun casting long stark shadows from the still bare cherry trees across the campus, when I swiped my library card a couple of times, struck yet again by its black-and-white photo of a bearded perpetual student out of Russian fiction, and headed underground to make some notes.

The acquisition policy of the university is a curious one. Professors are entitled to order any books they feel they require for their research or personal interest. These volumes are registered and then returned to the purchasers to keep in their offices until retirement, at which point the entire collection of a lifetime's curiosity and study is deposited in the stacks. As a result, you can find the most eccentric publications. And, I freely admit it, I feel at home down there. One of my pastimes is imagining new systems for cataloguing acquisitions. There's the seven-handshake system, the strange bedfellows system, the occult influence system ... but I digress.

Yes, one of those warm days near winter's end, when you feel you're about to be born, or reborn at least – that was the day when, as fate would determine, I picked out the *Death's Jest Book* volume of Thomas Lovell Beddoes's *Works* (I mean the two-volume 1928 edition dedicated to the memory of Edmund Gosse). Naturally enough I admired the binding, work of a quality long since vanished from the earth, and, blowing the dust from the top, gingerly opened its thick pages, not wanting to cause any damage to them if – as is so often the case down there – they haven't even been cut. Someone had certainly read the whole of this volume before, though, for there was no need to perform that curiously tantalizing chore. Just as I was reaching the section that most interested me in this neglected poet's works, my eye alighted on a faded blue envelope lying upon the matt lino floor at the foot of the stack.

It must have fallen out of the book, I thought, stooping down to pick it up. That letter certainly hadn't been there when I ambled down between the still-moving shelves. The envelope was addressed to the visiting professor of English by title but not name, and it had been rather hurriedly torn open. Inside was a letter closely written, but on one side only, of five pale blue sheets. The top one bore the single-line address, 'as from Land's End', and it was dated in the month of the Wall Street Crash.

'Dear Charley,' it began, 'your letter came a week ago and I'm afraid it left me feeling even worse about our prospects than ever ...' I know it's not right to look at letters that aren't meant for your eyes only, but I just couldn't help myself, and read the missive through twice, from the 'Dear Charley' to the 'Your own Marian'. It was an extremely personal letter – one detailing the difficulties of their life together. She had travelled alone, it appeared, halfway round the world to be with him here, going by ship through the Suez Canal, then across the Indian Ocean, and the China Sea ... finally to land at the port of Nagasaki. Marian had then found herself in this strange country, unable to speak the language, to shop or do anything but cook and wait for this Charles whatever-his-name-was to come back from his office. There was a long paragraph in which she enumerated her sorrows, her loneliness and solitude, the difficulty making friends, especially among the town's miniscule expatriate community of American missionaries and educationalists. It went on to apologize for her embarrassing tearfulness in public, her feeling that she had let herself down – and him too, with her painful regret and sense of failure. It was hard enough to read it through, even though her words were not addressed to me. I couldn't help wondering how this Charles had received it, and how it had come to be left in the pages of *Death's Jest Book*. Marian's letter made it clear that their winter together in the foreign professor's traditional-style house, perched on a mountain not far from the ruins of its ancient castle, had been a terribly cold one. Surviving it, Marian had finally come to the conclusion that the only way to save herself from a nervous breakdown, and to mend her marriage, was to spend some time back home on the family's West Penwith estate. She had added in a postscript that she was so sorry her ship had left Yokohama on Saint Valentine's Day – which was such a bad omen, but so it had been.

This peering into other peoples' sorry love lives, and not just as if you weren't there, had practically made me blush down between the concertina stacks, and my first thought – unrealistic as could be – was that the letter must be returned to its sender or, better, recipient. But how would I ever do that? It was dated 1929, an age ago now, and the best I could even hope would be to return it to the copyright holders of the recipient's literary estate, assuming, that is, that this Charles had such an archive somewhere.

Perhaps it was only because my name also happens to be Charles – people call me Charlie – but the natural researcher in me was fired by these tantalizing details from the life of one of my predecessors in this out of the way job as a teacher of literature to the youth of Northern Japan. You see, this particular university had a tradition going back to just after the Great War of inviting published poets to work as its foreign professors, so, more than likely, this Charles had been a poet too – and if I could find out what his surname was, I might be able to discover whether he and his Marian had managed to save their marriage, whether he did have literary executors, or an archive anywhere, and then return this sad document to its rightful place, its rightful library, as it were.

❧

As I say, I've never got used to the invisible feeling that goes with this position, and being among fellow aliens, as I sometimes inevitably am, doesn't, I'm afraid, tend to help much either. In a hotel lobby as the drinks take hold, they'll be laughing fit to burst, tears falling from their faces, laughing till it seemed they would come to pieces, splitting their sides, as if undone. Of course, they'll have their resident comedian. He'll be running through his repertoire of different gags and voices, evoking the past in a turn of lip or phrase. Yet it must be admitted he'll do no more than provide them with excuses. The things he says are funny, but no more than the truth.

'Sorry about the state I'm in,' he might interject, shaking the glass in his fist as if suffering from DTs, then using one of the hand-towels to wipe up the few stray spills slopped onto the table.

'What state is that?' his straight man would ask.

'Japan.'

'Enough in itself to drive you to drink!' another will say, gripping the tiny glass with two hands and desperately sucking another drop from his Kirin original lager, as if his life depended on it. And that would be enough to tip them all over the edge once more.

Perhaps I should explain. It will have been the sense of relief, hidden at last, as they might be, behind a row of dwarf palm trees. An assortment of old hands and new arrivals, thrown together by circumstance, they'll have seemed an odd crowd there in the not too antiseptic beige of that hotel lobby bar. Seven of them in all, they might be sitting on sofas in two rows of three with their comedian in residence, plus me, on a chair drawn up to one side.

The senior figure, the comedian's mentor it seemed, would be playing the central role. He might be on a lecture tour of the country, and being on tour can be reason enough, as some of them clearly understood, to be collapsing in helpless laughter. The professor's performance will have passed off without a hitch. After the applause and questions, he'll have been approached as he stepped from the podium, and asked to sign a couple of books surprisingly pushed towards him – including one written by somebody else, who happened to have the same name.

'Well now that's done: and I'm glad it's over,' he'll have quoted, approaching his support team in the foyer of the conference where the publishers lay out their wares. There was the need to care and not to care. There was, as some knew only too well, the need for a near complete self-effacement in living here … producing, as it did, an overwhelming sense of release when the effaced person was granted the chance to indulge this disappeared self among relatively like-minded others. Yet it seemed I could never make that work for me, could barely get a word in edgeways.

'It makes you feel two-faced,' the honoured guest would say.

'But why be two-faced when you can be many-faceted,' their resident comedian might quip.

'Touché,' the other would reply.

'The trouble is,' as the comic might explain, 'we're all forced to be two-faced here. It comes with the territory. Take, for example, this whole series of cases I'm painfully compelled to tell you every last detail of … where you're every time not only stabbed in the back, but must die the death of a thousand cuts.'

'And which simply obliges us to take an egoistic approach,' another would put in, 'because in fact we have no real purchase on any other reality.'

'Then they go and accuse you of being ungrateful,' as a third might say.

'Not untrue anywhere,' the lecture tourist could murmur.

Now the comedian, as it turns out, is telling his jokes from the challenged self-esteem of the professional artist whose livelihood depends on breaking down the resistance of even the most frozen of audiences – which, in this case, means the young woman sitting beside him, who appears (quite falsely) to be just such a difficult customer. It had, nevertheless, grown clear enough to this new presence, the only woman among their number, that here was a shower of those whinging Poms. Being new to the country, as she was, made her the implicit target for some of their advice-like talk. But such old-hands' tales are likely to pass the newcomers by, because perspectives and expectations are too far apart and, anyway, people must be allowed to make their own mistakes – education being an admirable thing, as Oscar Wilde says, though it is well to remember from time to time that nothing that is worth knowing can be taught.

Speaking of which, that's when I found myself trying to get a word in between their laughter, trying to tell them about this sad letter, the one fallen from that copy of *Death's Jest Book*, as you know, in the concertina stacks of our library. No, they were having none of it. Again it was like I couldn't make myself felt, as if someone had turned off my amplification. That melancholy missive was, in any case, way off topic for this band of aliens laughing fit to burst. Nothing could prevent them chattering on, interrupting each other with more and more of their nonsense, till, on the margins of that marginal group, I couldn't tell whether they were crying with laughter, or laughing through their tears.

❧

But back on campus, a few days later, it struck me that even if no one else was interested I would have to, for my own peace of mind, try and track this Charles whoever-he-was down. After all, it could turn out to be a regular *Big Clock*-style investigation. With nothing else in the world to do, as it happened, I couldn't help thinking that now was as good a time to start as any. There were bound to be archives on the history of the place, the yearbooks of defunct literary societies and such like ... and plenty of it here among the dusty scrolls and tomes.

Flicking over the pages of one yearbook after another, scanning down the columns of names and passport-style photographs, reading the minutes of societies and meetings, my capacity for obsession re-engaged, I saw flash before my eyes, as they say happens when you're drowning, like silent newsreel footage, the flickering images of what seemed to be someone else's life. I saw in the back of my mind's eye, as it were, a young man carrying a battered leather suitcase wandering through the old streets round Tokyo Station – a Tokyo Station looking like before the firebombs about a decade later. He's lost, it appears, and turning forlornly to left and right, till some Keystone-cop-like figures gather around an old wind-up telephone, followed by the arrival of a bowing and apologetic personage in spats.

Then these scenes cut to a Kabuki play, one with a curiously martial theme, for there are characters in army uniforms on stage, and beautifully painted sets of battle-field scenes. A little military band comes marching up to the footlights, and it's as if I can hear martial music and a patriotic song accompanied by traditional, stylized actions. Some young actors look like they're dressed as human bullets. Mothers and daughters smile proudly and wave to them. Though sections of the audience look half-asleep, at the end they all get to their feet, lift both hands into the air, and shout what must be 'Banzai', three times – 'Banzai, Banzai, Banzai'.

Then the scene changes to an open-air swimming pool on the side of a broad river. This young Charles appears in his swimming togs, shivering among a group of student figures. In fun, it must be, he's pushing a few of them into the water too. One of these students falls back with his arms raised in the air, like a redskin shot in a cowboy film. Then they push their foreign teacher in the water. He swims badly with a sort of doggy paddle. The students on the side of the pool look momentarily afraid he won't be able to get out again. They appear to be thinking of jumping in to save him. But, oddly enough, as I read on and picture these scenes I can feel a sort of embarrassment rising, as if it were myself in those images ashamed.

But now here he is again, alone, with the face of one thinking aloud. He's up to his ears under a brightly patterned futon cover, picking up manuscript scattered all over the bed, flicking over pages, then throwing them back in a heap. Passing outside are mothers and babies, bicycles, taxis, and crowds of street vendors. His face is a mask of anxiety. His hands are shaking. He seems to be trying to write a letter, scrunching up sheet after sheet and tossing them onto that traditional-style *tatami* floor.

Then another cut and there's one more futon beside his with a sleeping Asian girl under its blanket. Suddenly the camera starts shaking and shelf-loads of books come tumbling down. The two of them scramble to their feet, dithering about in that shuddering room. After some hasty dressing and more telegraphed exchanges of words, she runs out of the house, through the tree-filled garden. He follows her further into the street and they try to hail a taxi. One stops and the girl gets in, leaving the young foreigner to step back into that garden with its strangely wavering trees.

Now he's walking under high river cliffs with traditional houses built right up to their edges, precariously teetering over the drop. Then the woman from the earthquake scene turns up again. She's pleading with him about something, wringing her hands, with tears in her eyes. Her performance is fond and pathetic – so much so that I'm practically blushing myself. This Charley is trying to reassure her, it seems, and the whole scene is like nothing so much as a duet from *Madame Butterfly*.

And so it goes on, like a silent movie running in my head without those frames of written dialogue that cue the takes. And as I was researching further in the library basement archives, the flickering images and pictures moved to what looks like an enormous residence in the British Embassy. There are conversations with diplomatic types over tea round a table in its garden, a servant bringing in plates of scones. This Charles is introduced to someone who looks like a plotter in Hitchcock's *Secret Agent*. Then come inter-cut scenes of liberals and leftists being arrested, other suspicious-looking foreigners watched by secret policemen with gold-rimmed glasses.

Then there are flashes of this Charles with that parody spy going into the house from the earthquake scenes, where he's offered a room of his own. There are gestures of warning and concealment of papers. The revolutionary's wild arm-waving talk cuts to a scene with him being interrogated by army officers in a tiny cell. He's been stripped of his clothes and put into prison garb. Then there's a trial scene, with the man from the British Embassy leading the dissident, still in prison garb, out onto the swarming streets. Back in his house, this Charles of mine provides the spy, if that's what he is, with a change of clothes and theatrical disguise. Then we're in the docks at Yokohama, our Charles, the spy, and the man from the Embassy. Japanese secret policemen approach them. They present the spy with the clothes taken from him when he'd been interrogated. They are neatly cleaned and pressed.

Which is how it was that all the time I read on in the library basement, such images flickering before my mind's eye, faint bells were ringing in my head. But the odd thing was that when I checked again on a full list of foreigners who had held this post, it turned out only one of them was christened Charles and – you might think it a strange coincidence – he had the same surname too (though it's such a common or garden one that there could quite easily have been two of us). What's more, the list couldn't have included the two or three most recent professors because the information was printed in the back of a particular yearbook dated a couple of decades back now. Naturally, I assumed my university wouldn't include details of the present holder in its records, not until that person's contract had been *finally* terminated.

But studying the names of those foreigners who had held the same position, and following up traces of my namesake's case, it got me thinking that maybe more than one of them must have died in harness. So would they have been buried here, or been granted a mortuary passport and repatriated in their coffins or as flasks of ashes? Studying an old map of the city led me to the Buddhist temple with its adjacent graveyard in which land was given over to the burial of expatriate corpses. In a fit of sympathetic piety, I decided on another of those late winter afternoons to wander over and see what it was like. It turned out this particular Buddhist temple had been located on a hill some distance from the centre, right next to where, it turned out, they were putting through a new ring road.

At first it looked like any other temple. There were the ornamental-roofed buildings, a pagoda, and a garden with an island of paradise in it, reached by a row of what looked like stepping-stones. There was the usual Buddhist graveyard. You know how it is: Shinto for weddings, Buddhist for funerals. So picking my way along the rings of stones, the ash from incense sticks, and mini-cans of Asahi beer ornamenting their pediments, I came of a sudden to the limit of the graveyard. It ended beyond a screen of bamboo trees, in a sudden drop, a cliff-face of raw earth and rock chopped out so they could widen the highway directly into town. But had they destroyed any sections of that old burial ground? Would my attempt to find the letter's addressee end thus in disappointment? Glancing at each stone in turn, I was beginning to lose heart.

But I needn't have worried, for here they were, along a rising slope some distance further off, a row of great marble tombs with inscriptions in English. So I set to studying each and every one, until, right near the end, there, there it was: *Charles Smith 1902-1938 Requiescat in Pace*. And there it was: my own familiar name. Believe me, it felt like I'd discovered my own grave.

~

But, if so, what on earth had become of me? How then had I died? Back I went to the university archives for a further trawl along shelves and through boxes. In a folder at the bottom of one such box was a file of medical reports from the local hospital. They told how this Charles Smith, my namesake or double, had fallen ill with some undiagnosed condition involving headaches, hearing loss, balance problems, difficulty swallowing and other things besides. The doctors hadn't been able to identify the cause of his rapid decline. They'd been treating him with morphine simply to dull the symptoms. For months, it seemed, he had hung between life and death, till finally the scales had tipped and his vital chain snapped. So had he died of a broken heart? No doctor diagnoses heartbreak any more. Had Marian been aware of his plight? Evidently his ashes had not been repatriated and mingled with those of his lost Esmeralda. But what, for that matter, had become of his beloved, gone to recover from their miserable winter, at Penwith in the far west of England? Understandably enough, my researches into that, out here on the far aside of the globe, drew nothing but a blank.

And I had to admit it could happen: the researcher's capacity for obsession may get the better of him. You can sometimes become so wrapped up in your subject that you start to resemble your topic, to lose a sense of where your own life ended and his began. Yes, I had to admit it: it was as if I had been suffering from post-mortem amnesia, suffering from it all this time. Yet now, at least, I had an idea of the life I might have led and how it could have ended, all this way from anywhere that such a person as this Charles Smith might want to call a home.

On the subject of home, the archives did in fact reveal his residence, and another day I walked over to see what it was like. At the point where a wave of pine trees turned beyond a rusty iron fence, again I could picture that wooden house with blue corrugated iron roof, its stairwell stained with dampness, a casual spill, or shrivelled leaf here and there as if to chill the heart. Their sleeping quarters had been a single room perched on the roof. The risen sun would move across its frayed *tatami* floor. There were souvenirs of elsewhere on its walls. But none of what they came to know, none of *that* was there any more. It had all been bulldozed flat. First they'd been exiled from their exile; then years back it must have been condemned, demolished. Now as I stood by where the gate once was, gazing across an empty building plot, it appeared as if those years had never been.

Still, every now and then, I will come back to the old places, the rusted swings and sandpit where other aliens' children must have played. Drifting down those broad avenues, going the rounds of their old haunts, the house where my *doppelgänger* lived all those years before, the restaurants and bars that he would have visited, the bandstand out in the rain ... or floating towards the haunted suicides' bridge, the bridge across its gorge, naturally enough I might see coming towards me some other poor old wandering ghost. On that particular occasion it would be another of the foreign schoolteachers ... and though he too drifted past me as if I weren't there, as if he couldn't have been himself, by then a ghost character too, at least I had an explanation now for why he behaved that way.

I never did discover, though, if Charles Smith had an archive anywhere, or, as I say, what happened to Marian. And, after a while, as that state of obsession died down, I did wonder what I should do with her letter. Which is how, one lunchtime a little while later, I came to descend into the library basement once more, made my way to the same closed shelves, pressed the lighting up button, and slipped down between them, to replace that blue envelope in exactly those same pages of the very same volume of *Death's Jest Book* where it could remain till a later Beddoes fan would come along and find it there.

However, if you were to go there now, perhaps in search of that very same letter, you would find the access rules have changed. Now in the bowels of the library, if you look for the concertina stacks where I would browse, you're sure to find many people searching along the shelves, taking note of titles, checking quotations, all the things you would expect. Now, you see, graduate students too are allowed to go down and look at the library's holdings. You might say the stacks feel as if they have been exorcised.

A Mystery Murder

I wonder what got into me. Why did I accept the invitation? Mortally wounded *amour propre*, most likely. After all the years of struggle and indifference, when finally an invitation comes, what was I supposed to do? The other invitees were to be writers and critics whom I had either abused out of earshot, or else in print. Some of them had stabbed me in the face in articles, columns, or reviews, and, nothing could stop me speculating, behind and in my back as well. There was likely to be that magazine editor who had serially rejected my work. There would be members of interview committees, reporters on manuscripts for publishers, and figures from the prize club. There was sure to be the critic who'd stolen my ideas, every one of them, and not a word of acknowledgement in his footnotes. I must have been mad to say I would. Our host, the notable poet-critic, had once interviewed for a job I desperately needed. It could even have saved my second marriage. All right, I know: but it might have given it a third or fourth chance. Still, when he came out as the successful candidate, I immediately took steps to leave the country. There's only so much you can take.

But now he was inviting me back, into his haunt, as it were. It was to be a brainstorming session, a high-level get-together, something of that sort: thirteen characters gathered round a conference table, being expected to thrash out the state of things, as if it were a matter of life and death. But whose life and whose death? Sleep-walking out of a fourteen-hour flight, I was feeling like the thirteenth invited as I made myself known at the porter's lodge, followed her directions across a couple of quads, and found my semi-luxurious guest room. It was up two flights of narrow turning stairs.

The view from the row of high-arched windows was of the splendid variety. It extended across meadows in all their summer glory, meadows guarded and overlooked by ancient oaks, as far as the slowly sliding glint of the distant river that gave this place its name ...

'Just look at this venerable pile —' I'd exclaimed on first entering its great front quad, '— of shite!' said the pre-jaded wag beside me; and indeed there were drawbacks to being educated in such surroundings.

So here I was back in my old alma mater! The surface facts didn't seem changed at all. Yet for the time I stayed in that spacious tall-windowed guestroom, it was like I was living with the ghost of a person I might have been. It was somebody sulking by a marble faun, or outside a jolly corner restaurant. Then, as that feeling came back more strongly, I recalled having tried, a few years back now, to squeeze a tad of fellow feeling from one of my old drinking pals.

'The slights don't ever really heal,' I admitted. 'I'm scarred for life.'

'Oh get over yourself ... and move on like the rest of us,' came back his tart reply.

Down across its local version of the Bridge of Sighs, out for my usual pre-breakfast constitutional, so useful for their moments of inspiration or vision, I headed for the meadows beyond the college's long oak drive. Here were the old signs of so many murderous histories those trees had indifferently witnessed: civil wars, popular risings, and nights of long knives; and here was I back again in the checkered shade of the sandy towpath's tree-shaped shadows.

No need to hurry, no one caring if I lived or died – or so I thought. I could take my time about it, dawdling along to make each moment stretch out like those sharp-edged shadows. Ahead were the college boathouses set back from the river's brink, their activities getting under way, individual oarsmen and women bearing the pointed boats above their heads, frail craft which would float them out on the current, as if to make me quote and remember.

This early down the river, then, an oarsman was backing fast into his morning while a bike-rider with megaphone was bellowing words of advice. Another emblem there! Here the ones doing it couldn't even see where they were going, while the others, out of their element, were giving advice about how it should be done. There would always be that possibility of the coach on his bike riding smack into a tree, as if in *Carry On Studying* or *Gone with the Window*, but that didn't look likely to happen as both of them sped on round the bend.

❧

Whodunnit fashion, we didn't have a shortage of candidate victims, this thirteen of us to be precise – and all with a portfolio of reasons to be bumped off. There was our host, the quintessential poet-critic, his love handles turning to middle age spread. There was our Internet magazine founder, all pixels and dpi numbers, suffering from permanent headaches and eyestrain. The print journal editor, who naturally looked down on the virtual reality man, wore shades, and handed out subscription flyers like junk bonds going out of fashion. The jobbing reviewer had deadlines to meet, and would slip off to his room intent on converting the press release into an original article. There was our short-story writer with a twinkle in his eye – no, not me, I'm just trying my hand at the genre, typing out whatever comes into my head. The grand dame of verse had deigned to put in an appearance (between an Australian prize judging and a guest lecture in Finland). The professional nationalist was here with his holier-than-thou fringe benefits. There was a career feminist, of course, properly irate about being in a minority of two. Naturally the permanent writer-in-residence barely knew where his next meal was coming from, and indeed had to get back to a sheaf of grant applications. The academic hitman was escaping from some poor fool's graduate thesis turned book-proposal lined up in his sights. The exhausted head of department was in need of a haircut, a style-rethink, and a ten-year sabbatical to get those skeletons out of his cupboard. Then there was our American scholar, fresh from a formalists-versus-free-verse symposium, full of the latest manifestos and agendas. The London literary man about town would be writing up our little get-together for his weekly column, while the story's narrator, me myself I, had been flown in from another time zone for reasons as yet to be revealed, or revealed to me, at least.

Of course, these were all kind-of-colleagues and, one or two of them, almost I might have said friends. Down there on my pre-breakfast walks, it was as if they had all combined with the host's pressed invitation to give me a moment's pause. Past flaked edges, undulant willows, equivocal bends and shallows, I might just have the chance to pull that past together, roll it up into a ball, like some failed draft, and chuck the lot right into that glinting intellectual waterway. Then those past-resented years might become a blur and be lost in so many forgotten opportunities, leaving me able to see again untarnished the clouds among leaf-fringes, the shimmer of sunlight on water, and all those other far-off things.

❧

Being out of the loop – and how – I wasn't finding it at all easy to catch on to what the others were discussing. The topics of conversation in any such microclimate shift as unpredictably as the weather in this north European archipelago. The prizewinners come and go with the publishing seasons, each receiving their due portions of resentment and bile. Attempts to link by direct analogy the current styles with equally current burning issues and persuasions could only hold conviction for the weeks that were a long time in politics or, for that matter, literature written for the moment. After all my years away in a species of exile, I hardly knew the names of the players, never mind what games they were playing.

Ever the tactless unbeliever, I would slip up in the brain storming sessions themselves.

'We murder to dissect,' said the poet-critic at our first bout, 'if I may quote a phrase.'

'Live dissections have been reported in certain experimental conditions,' I put in with a loaded inflection.

'You're not comparing us to concentration camp doctors?' asked the man about town, with his familiar politesse.

'Absolutely not,' I said, 'just trying to lighten up the session here, folks.'

And at those agonizing moments with their seminar eyes all turned upon me, as I coughed to get into one exchange about something or other, I could see it in their faces. It was obvious to me at least. I was to be the chosen victim, as clearly as if I'd been tied to a stake with the big black stewpot heating up below me. 'If one of you doesn't get your just desserts first,' I had to prevent myself saying out loud.

'It'll be just another case of *Ars longa, vita brevis*,' the academic hitman would smilingly say, and apropos of what seemed nothing.

After the first few sessions, it was true, I could sense that from various quarters of the room, people were going out of focus, their voices falling silent. The short story writer, occasionally scrawling a note of some kind on the back of the programme, hadn't said a thing for some hours. Like the Cheshire cat – who was from hereabouts too – the granddameofversehaddisappeared.Whateverhadhappened to her?

'She just had to split early,' our host explained.

So that was one name to cross off my list.

'But isn't it supposed to be enjoyable?' said the Internet magazine founder. 'Art, I mean ... isn't it supposed to be enjoyable?'

This was in response to a rallying call from the poet-critic inviting us to make more strenuous moral enquiry into the ideals of disinterested contemplation. I'm afraid to confess my tummy rumbled even as he spoke.

The college food was, it has to be admitted, no worse than could be expected; we were lucky not to have been mysteriously poisoned, one and all. Breakfast was taken, for those that could stomach it, among gaggles of the senior citizens there for a gerontology conference. Three-course lunches were held in a common room, allowing conversations with neighbours to escape from the official topics on our programme, but equally putting paid to much intellectual effort once the dishes had been ingested.

Dinners were served on the undergraduate benches in college hall ...

❧

But it was the evenings in the pub afterwards when my being out of the loop was most painfully revealed. It was when the so-called state of things actually got thrashed out too. As soon as we'd settled down to our first drinks, while the laughter and gossip began to circulate, one or other celebrity's name would never be far from somebody's teeth.

'He's had it now,' the academic hitman might say.

'Oh, she'll get what she deserves,' said the professional feminist.

'So-and-so's totally shot,' said the nationalist poet.

'Well, I didn't know there was a backlash going on against such-and-such-a-one,' I naively blurted out.

'A backlash?' said one of the survivors. 'There hasn't even been a front-lash, as far as I'm concerned.'

'God, I could kill him,' said the head of department.

'Why?' our token woman, the professional feminist, now reduced to the role of love interest, glumly enquired.

'Because he's gone and taken my name in vain!'

'Oh, calm down, we all of us have a more famous crime writer with just the same handle,' said the perpetual writer-in-residence.

'If we don't have a pop star as well,' I said – me myself I.

Naturally, my fellow-talkers had it in for the usual suspects; but if, like me, you haven't the time or patience to keep up with the review and letters pages of the weekly journals, let alone the quarterlies and little magazines, it's not that easy to tell whom the usual suspects might be.

Being out of everything, anyway, you don't have a lot of evidence for thinking that other people are expressing opinions behind your back, and indeed the more likely thought is that you're being treated to the usual non-benign neglect. However, as those talking shops continued, I began to pick up the occasional hint, and actually started to wonder whether I wasn't myself being suspected of something – if not quite yet counted among those usual suspects to be rounded up by the thought police.

Needless to say, I've done my fair share of hatchet jobs ... and the problem with these kinds of symposia, as I soon discovered, was that they resembled nothing so much as a trial by jury, a jury of your victims. We were all expected to come face to face with our corpses and accusers and then discuss the niceties of analogous cases and crimes with precisely those same people.

The overworked head of department was next to disappear, and no need to ask what had finished him off. I sadly deleted his name from my list.

So there we were, involved, after hours of shiftless searching for some common ground, in the delicate question of whether any of these little crimes should even be so much as mentioned. Would anyone or anything ever be brought to book for the decimation that had occurred, a decimation of which this was no more than a sideshow? I had long since abandoned all hope.

By the next-to-last day, though, I settled on the policy of admitting to everything – even the things I hadn't done. That way no one would accuse you of anything else, or so I thought.

'I'm so sorry,' I said, to one of my victims, 'if those words of mine did cause you pain. Mind you, we *are* paid to say what we honestly think, are we not?'

I even found myself apologizing for the case where I'd been credited with a book review filed by another of the suspects. It was none of my doing, and you know how it is with newspapers. They hadn't even printed a correction and apology. I was sorry, but that didn't make the hate mail for his character assassinations any less painful to receive.

And what of the ten other victims remaining? Would I still have to pick one? Just one? Would a thought experiment do the trick of assuaging my thirst for ... for what exactly was it? I was saying this to myself as I tried to access my e-mail in the student computer room. Sitting at the screen beside mine was the American academic, firing off messages to the @marks on his global network. I'd been granted a couple in my time. He was capable of sending acceptances and rejections of manuscripts in seven keystrokes, initials included. Now that's what I call efficient dispatch.

Later the same day he took a little more time to explain over a drink exactly what was wrong with one of my more recent publications. What it amounted to was that I had dared to express a limiting judgment about the father professor who had taken him under an extended wing and helped him to a tenure-track post somewhere in the desert places of the south-by-south-west. I found his unexpressed loyalty almost touching in its creaturely gratitude. Needless to say, I attended to his arguments – ones being shouted at me over the beer-hall foreground noise – about how my premises were way wrong, how my conclusions should be less drastic ...

'God, I could murder you,' I thought, and smiled my most open-minded of smiles.

At the dinner to celebrate our symposium's end, there was certainly relief at having reached that far without any actual bloodshed. Even here, though, our host had failed to appear. Had he been imagining all this time that we would bond better without his oversight, by giving us the chance to talk about him behind his back? If so, his ears couldn't have been burning. We disposed of him with that old quip: 'If there's one thing worse than being talked about ... it's being not talked about.' Still, there were a few comic moments at our would-be feast of mirth – like the sight of an entire fellowship trying to fight its way into an *hors d'oeuvre* of unripe avocadoes. Some were chewing manfully at the flakes they had chipped off, while others were pushing them disgustedly away, as if at a dinner staged by that multi-person Portuguese writer what's-his-face.

As we chattered about this and that, the absent, indeed, seemed on or near everyone's lips. Naturally, we did mention in passing the two characters we had lost along the way. Among the others were family members missed back home, with whom the participants were itching to be reunited. Since the death of my parents and the inevitable divorce that came as a result of my expatriation, I have barely any to speak of. So that excuse for my disappearance did not arise. If I could survive the last night's drinking, I would be heading back to the airport first thing the following morning and subjecting myself to one more long-haul flight.

Darkened oil paintings of the immortal dead in broad gilded frames were pointedly ignoring us from the high-panelled walls. They were the usual mixed bunch of great poets and scholars who had helped to create the very language we were speaking, most of their names lost in the mists of information overload – though able to be looked up should the need arise. There was the one with the eye-patch like a buccaneer, another with skin the colour of Stilton cheese, a third whose reputation for obscure sexual practices had recently eclipsed the renown of his overwhelming lyric gift. Some of their names were practically there on the tips of our tongues. But most of us were pointedly paying them back by pretending they weren't there too.

'Yes, it seems we're all on the point of ...', one of our number began on the side opposite me.

Now was my moment! With all our survivors gathered together and in something resembling festive mood, now was the time to do it pat! That's exactly what I was thinking as I gingerly slipped a hand into my inside pocket, feeling around for the murder weapon, but where had it got to? Where was my poisoned blue pencil?

'Don't do it,' said a voice beside me; but she was clearly talking to somebody else – about whether to accept a memorial volume commission, or so it appeared. Well, of course, of course you've already guessed that I didn't do it; I didn't do anything of the kind. We really didn't deserve it, did we? No, a murder's just too good for the likes of us. That's what I found myself thinking. Far too good, wouldn't you say? It would make all this typing have a point, would make it approach a satisfactory end. *Ut doceat* and all that ...

Yet there at this pause in the flagging conversation, as I looked up from the ruins of the meal on my plate, and around at the dining hall table, the din in the room for a moment stilled, as if for a parting grace, or *coup de grâce*, it seemed there was really nobody to kill, we were all as good as dead already; or at least that there was, and had been for some time, an intangible corpse amongst us, the lifeless body of the real victim there in our midst.

Foreigners, Drunks and Babies

'In fact the whole of Japan is a pure invention. There is no such country, there are no such people.'
Oscar Wilde, *The Decay of Lying*

'The welcome party is on Wednesday night. Will Mrs James come too?' The department assistant, Mr Sato, had half-turned from his computer screen. It showed the homepage of a second-hand book store.

'Certainly I will. Looking forward. Not sure about my wife, though.'

I *was* sure, in fact. As if to acknowledge what was thought to be a custom in the outside world, my Head of Department would regularly let it be known that resident wives of visiting professors were very welcome to go through the ordeal of such official get-togethers. But Gillian, my wife, had realized soon after coming to live here that foreigners' *gaijin* spouses were not really expected to attend such events.

'Professor Yoneyama has decided we will go somewhere special,' Mr Sato was saying, 'and I have booked a Chinese restaurant down town.'

'Great,' I said. 'By the way, how's it going?'

Mr Sato gave a slight wince by way of an answer. His doctoral dissertation on *The Invisible Man* was causing him acute compositional anguish. I expressed a few visiting professorial noises to the effect that I was standing by to correct his English the moment that was needed. It was early October, the week of the second semester's intensive course. Mr Sato's submission date was fast approaching. His barely-started thesis would not be ready for examination in this academic year.

'What's Professor Miyazaki talking about?' I asked.

'*Much Ado about Nothing*,' said Sato.

I made a mental note to think of something halfway

sensible to ask about the translation of Dogberry's speeches in Japanese.

Twice a year the department hosted a weeklong special lecture during which regular classes would be cancelled. The students were given a break from the usual voices and a glimpse of someone else's teaching. Professor Satoshi Miyazaki, one of the best young Shakespeareans in the country, had come up from Kyoto to fill out the department's coverage that year. Toshi and I were one-time colleagues in the old capital. Despite my transfer to this university, a four-hour Bullet Train journey away, we had managed to keep up our acquaintance and met occasionally at conferences in far-flung parts of the country.

'Will you be going to the second party?' Mr Sato asked.

'Don't know,' I thought it best to reply. 'My wife's got a bad cold and isn't sleeping well – I may have to get home early.'

'You are a doting husband,' said Sato.

But I was only too aware of using my wife's health as a cast-iron excuse for going home after the first party had ended. By then the wilder students would already be turning bright pink, yelling at the tops of their voices, challenging each other to drinking contests, getting so drunk they'd be on the verge of collapse. Years back now, when a third-year student, Sato himself had committed the embarrassing act of mixing his drinks at the annual welcome party and, dead drunk, had been convulsively sick all over the foreign professor. Immediately, a group of girl students – like trainee mothers with a wayward baby – had taken charge of the very pale Sato, cleaned him up, walked him around, then helped him back to the tiny student hole he rented. Others had brought water and warm cloths to sponge the half-digested food and drink from their foreign professor's grey flannel suit. Momentarily inclined to be annoyed, I quickly found myself appreciating the funny side – not least because Sato would be crippled with shame in class the next day. It would be something that I'd have over him, or so he would think, for the rest of his university career. And what a career! Sato had gone from the ridiculous to the sublime, had risen from his drunken exploit to being the department assistant with an MA in American fiction, a year's experience researching in a college in Washington State, and three essays published in local academic journals. With the doctorate completed, he would surely be an unstoppable candidate for a post in the shrinking and ever more competitive Japanese assistant professorial market.

Autumn was the conference season, season of talks and visiting lectures. Having carved a niche out for myself up here, I didn't much like watching foreigners new to the country stumble ineptly all over my patch. But as chance would have it, this year the invitee being Toshi, the Wednesday night party at the Chinese restaurant promised to be a chance to catch up on news and gossip from Western Japan. I was almost excited by the thought of going.

Come Wednesday, the various dishes kept arriving, the Lazy Susan in the centre slowly revolving, and I kept racking my brains for something else to say. I had found myself placed between two of the quietest graduate girls. Pretty they were, but their lack of conversational skills would have given shrinking violets and wallflowers the reputations of brazen hussies. This, frankly, was the only problem with these department gatherings, the problem of what to say.

'Dr James, I know you are a scholar,' Miyazaki had asked me when we'd first met, 'but what exactly is your academic field? Who is your specialist subject?'

On that occasion it was me lost for an answer. If only I had done, all those years before, what the sensible graduate students did: chosen a canonical author with a large oeuvre that I could devote my entire life to re-editing and discussing in ever-greater depth. But I had always preferred the life of the hit-and-run merchant who finds a poet with a writing-block, the sort who finally ends up producing a slim *Collected Poems* after a life of obscurity and neglect. With authors like that you could knock off the essay rediscovering them, get it published in a quarterly somewhere, then, without so much as a look back after the proof-stage, move on to your next accident-statistic.

'Well – actually – poetry,' I said with a defensive smile.

'Ah,' my new acquaintance Dr Miyazaki had returned, 'so you do not have a specialist field.'

'No, I suppose I don't,' I admitted, to nip that toxic topic in the bud.

Not furnishing him with expected answers may have been what made him seek me out, though. Certainly our acquaintance had blossomed, and was now one of many years' standing.

'So what are you teaching in your classes this semester?' he asked. The graduate girl with a voice like a disappearing mosquito had been asked by Professor Yoneyama to change places so Toshi could have a word with his old acquaintance. She had done so with a cringing bow.

Given the requirement was to teach six classes, usually described in the course handbooks as either *Reading* or *Conversation*, there were, in effect, no restrictions on what you could teach. So the question did have a point, and would reveal a thing or two about the interests of the person to whom it was asked. The problem with my answer, however, was that since Toshi hadn't read any of the obscure poets I was introducing to my students that autumn, the conversation faltered and died right there. So he graciously offered me one of the new dishes heaving into view on the revolving platform. I took another sip of my Asahi Dry.

'What's Brook doing with my old job?' I asked, to start another patch of conversation.

'He left the country earlier this year,' is exactly what Toshi then replied.

'What about his wife?' I asked. 'Has she gone with him? The last I heard she had an assistant's post at the Buddhist University ...'

'I can't say.'

But why did the mention of Aiko always seem to produce such blank absences of news or information? I couldn't say I hadn't noticed it before.

'She had a junior lectureship there,' said Toshi, 'but I never knew her.'

'So what's Brook doing then? Is he on leave?' I asked, thinking this might at last hit a vein of gossip that, with the inebriation, could kick-start a bit of an exchange.

Alan Brook, another of Professor Sakai's recruits who had come to teach in Toshi's department, was Aiko's husband. Concerned about her welfare as Finals and Graduate School entrance approached, I had introduced them about ten years before, when about to leave for a vacation with Gill back in Islington.

'He always kept to himself,' said Toshi, with a more than usually expressionless look. 'I don't know what he is doing.'

'Yes,' I came back, warming to the theme, 'Professor Sasayama said a very true thing about their mysterious relationship. What they had in common, he said, was that neither is good at either making or keeping friends. Don't you think that's exactly right? I haven't heard a thing from them for two or three years now.'

'You don't know?' He had leant towards me and lowered his voice to a whisper.

'Know what?' I asked.

'She died.'

The vein of genial gossip turned to ice within me. The sociable meal around us had been cast into a distant relief.

'How? What happened? Was it a car crash? Or what?'

'She killed herself,' said Toshi with the very same absence of feeling that in this case seemed to express his reluctance to talk.

'Why? What for? When did it happen?'

'In the middle of September.'

Five weeks ago, I thought, and no one had thought to tell me.

'How? How come?'

'She hanged herself with a scarf,' said Toshi.

'But why?' I asked, incredulous. 'Everything was going so well for her: the marriage, the baby, the doctorate, and a permanent job to cap it all ...'

'I cannot say any more,' Toshi answered, distinctly uncomfortable, 'not here.'

I must have looked horror-struck, visibly upset both by the bare fact and lack of an explanation.

'After my course finishes ... tomorrow,' he added, 'perhaps I may come to your office?'

As promised, Toshi Miyazaki knocked at my brown metal door sometime a little after five the following afternoon. Moving a heap of books and papers down to a still empty space on the floor, I offered him a department leatherette armchair.

'I don't know a lot about it,' he said, after a word or two on how his course had gone. 'I'm head of the teaching committee this year, and the Dean phoned me to say that

Brook had resigned his post – because his wife died. It was just two weeks before the start of the semester. The Dean asked me to organize some part-time teaching to make up the students' credits. It was most inconvenient, most inconsiderate of him.'

There was nothing I could do with that. His Japanese wife had died, and he had left the country.

'So where's their daughter?' I asked, wondering about the extended family she had taken me to visit for the first of my Japanese New Years.

'She left the country with him.'

'But did you talk to Alan before he left, about what happened, I mean?'

'No,' said Toshi. 'It was the Dean who told me she had committed suicide.'

'But surely you spoke to Alan about his classes and that?'

'We spoke on the phone ... He said he didn't want to talk about the tragedy. He was seeing his lawyers in Tokyo, making arrangements to sell their property and leave Japan as quickly as possible ...'

'Where is he now, do you know?'

'I believe he has returned to Oxford – with the little daughter.'

'You don't happen to have an address for him by any chance, do you?'

'No – but I'm sure the Dean will have his contact details.'

'Perhaps I'll try and get in touch with him,' I said, not knowing where I'd begin or what I could possibly ask in a letter to a person who had barely confided in me at all.

Toshi Miyazaki had a Bullet Train to catch, and excused himself a few moments later, saying if I were passing through Kyoto that New Year I should get in touch – because, perhaps, he would know a little more by then.

So there I was standing in the middle of my chaos

trying to manage the mixture of upset and bafflement that Aiko's death had caused. She'd been the first to befriend me all those years before. It was almost immediately after I 'materialized myself' by the exit gate at Itami Airport in Osaka. That's what Sakai had asked me to do, and with that very verb. Alone in the country, with Gill remaining back home in North London to see how things developed, I was very short of company. My new colleagues seemed equally indifferent to my existence.

This had a history too. Professor Sakai, my recruiter in London, was not exactly popular with his fellow academics. One of the things they held against him was his lack of formal inhibition. He was notorious for saying things about colleagues that should, conventionally, only have been hinted at when everyone had imbibed enough saké to excuse the impoliteness or indiscretion. There was almost a set amount of drink that had to be downed before the conversation could loosen up, and only then on the strict understanding that anything said in that inebriated state would be treated the next morning as if nothing of the kind had been uttered, as if none of the evening's events had ever happened at all. The knack was, I finally realized, to manage your drink so as always to be slightly less drunk than those around you. That way you could learn a lot from the loose-tongued in your vicinity while rationing the drip-drip of gossip that would keep the flow alive.

There was, in fact, a large clique in the department that defined itself in precise opposition to Sakai and his manipulatively uninhibited ways. They tended to be the younger specialists in American literature, and regarded the older professor's promotion of British culture in the department as a reactionary harking back to the pre-war world of Edmund Blunden, Ralph Hodgson, William Empson and their like. My sponsor had, however, realized perfectly well that by being identified as the 'friend' of the British visiting professors he made it even more difficult for them to integrate with the rest of the department, and had warned me to be equally amicable and helpful to all, not to side with one faction or another on any single issue, and even to go out of my way to try and socialize with the younger crowd. But the net effect was that all of them left me entirely alone.

Aiko Mori had, at the very same time, come back from a year in America. She had been studying English in a small community college somewhere in Idaho. Now she was back in Kyoto for the final year of her Literature degree. Doubtless with the idea of keeping up her newly improved English, she had gone along to the native-speaking professor's first class in the Faculty of Arts. I remembered that familiar sinking feeling as it seemed there would be only two students enrolled on the course, one of whom, a silent boy, didn't seem able to answer the simplest of questions. Fortunately the other, the diminutive Aiko (so thin you could think if she turned sideways she'd disappear), was more than ready to respond – and with a frank enthusiasm I would come to understand was dangerously un-Japanese.

Adjourning to the Clark House café with my two Arts students, I was glad to hear Aiko explain the temporary timetable clash. That's how Aiko Mori came to occupy a peculiar place in my recessed affections. She'd befriended me when I felt totally alone. A shoebox among the office detritus contained some photos from those far-off Kyoto years.

'Do you think anyone else will come?' I had asked from the platform.

The two students glanced at each other.

'No, they will not,' said the philosophy major, with his air of pronouncing a fact.

'But it's not because of you,' Aiko immediately added. 'There's been a change in the schedule and many of the students won't be able to come now; but I know a few who will come next week.'

'I brought something for us to look at,' I said, 'but maybe it would be best then not to start just now. Why don't we get out of this horrible room and have a cup of tea somewhere, since there's only the three of us.'

'Good idea,' said Aiko, after the two students had exchanged another glance.

'Right,' I said, 'decided – but let me just write your names down in my register book.'

It was Aiko who suggested we go to the coffee house opposite the Italian Cultural Institute that morning. As I later discovered, there was a Kyoto *gaijin* witticism about how the Italian Institute was a café, the Alliance Française a restaurant, the Goethe Institute a concert hall, the British Council a language school, and the American Center a cover for the CIA ... But the Clark House, being right next to the Kyoto University campus, was to be the scene for many of our meetings. On that first day a waitress approached us and casually nodded a bow. I ordered a milk tea. The students ordered American coffee.

'So have you been abroad,' I asked, prompted by their order and the imitation boho surroundings.

The philosophy student, deferred to by Aiko, briefly shook his head.

'I was in the States last year,' said Aiko.

'Great,' I said. 'Whereabouts?'

'Idaho and California,' she replied.

'Great,' I repeated, and, conscious of cultivating her a little too enthusiastically, turned to the philosophy student to ask him a question about his interests in the field. The boy answered as best he could. Then I explained my plans for the year's over-ambitious course on Anglo-American poetry from Hopkins to Ashbery ... and expressed the hope that some more students would want to attend next week.

'Interesting,' said Aiko. 'But in England, what do the students call their professors?'

'Mostly by their first names,' I replied. 'Mine used to call me Robert. Some even called me Bob. But they usually call them "Dr So-and-so" if they don't know them, or are talking about them with another lecturer.'

'I think I'll call you "Dr B",' said Aiko, friendly and familiar from the start.

❧

The Inland Sea was one great natural, womb-like harbour, and Shiraishijima the third stop on the ferry route. When finally our boat cast off and we were chugging down the estuary, past a cluttered shoreline of ramshackle boatyards and derelict wharves, my spirits, as was usual on such short boat trips, immediately began to lift. Onboard were a few shoppers who'd gone to the mainland for supplies. There were some teenagers lolling in the stern: smoking, munching junk food, drinking from cans and throwing their litter straight over the side.

'And they like to think they love nature,' said Gill.

'The perpetual pursuit of dainty,' I said, quoting the slogan for a chain of coffee and cake shops, my mood continuing to improve as we reached the deceptively open sea.

'I blame the drinks dispensers,' said Gill, wrinkling her nose at the drift of smoke from the school kids in the stern. Her need to complain remained unsatisfied, but my lifting mood didn't want to go there – and I preferred instead to watch cargo boats passing between the islands.

The weather had turned vicious. It was freezing cold, with a rolling swell. Gill wasn't enjoying the buffeting either and had now gone to sit inside the cabin. I stood holding onto a rail towards the bow, letting the brief sea voyage do its work. Shiraishijima could be made out up ahead, already a spot on the far horizon.

The island turned out to be an oval of flat, cultivated ground ringed with an arch of steep hills. It was the remnant of a small volcanic cone. In the flat oval there were some narrow lanes of houses near the ferry port where we docked, lanes thinning out to a few tiny rice fields, seaweed-drying platforms and shellfish industries. The buildings were traditional, made of dark-stained wood, but not like the centre of Kyoto. They were poor, ramshackle-seeming, with a store or two and one tiny noodle shop which stood beyond the pier. There had to be a quarry somewhere in the ring of hills, for a lorry stood parked beside the dock loaded with pale stone slabs. Shiraishijima: White Stone Island, it meant.

Disembarked, its key collected from the ferry ticket office, we were making our way through those narrow streets towards the International Villa. The very existence of such an architect-designed residence on Shiraishijima was a further recent tribute to the rigid distinction between *inside* and *outside* that gave form to Japanese society. The local prefecture government had built this hostel as a friendly gesture to encourage *gaijin* – outside people – visitors. Though such a gesture might seem the opposite of exclusion, it reinforced the distinction in reverse. The prices were especially low, and Japanese people could not stay in the hostel unless accompanying foreigners. Sakai, my sponsor, always on the look-out for a bargain, had told me about them, and one time years back he'd arranged a trip to Ushimado – a fishing port on the Honshu coast of the Inland Sea, rather wishfully called the Japanese Aegean because of the clusters of islands and climate favouring the olive groves terraced up their hillsides. That stay was where the idea of visiting Shiraishijima had come from in the first place. Only this time the foreigners would make the arrangements and go under their own steam.

Not knowing the lie of the land brought its problems, of course. We had taken the ferryboat without supplies, imagining there would be the usual convenience stores on every other corner. But once landed on the tiny island, we found no restaurants, excluding the noodle shop by the harbour, and only two other stores of any kind. There was a fishing tackle place, no earthly use to us, and shut up it seemed for the winter, while the general store revealed its limitations both on the food and, more seriously, on the drink front. Gill had never taken to cooking Japanese vegetables, and we'd both eaten enough white rice for a lifetime. Still, we could make do in a pinch. But the drink and alcohol problem was chronic. There was a bottle of gin but no tonic, and the only orange was fizzy Fanta. There was coke, but no rum. There was neither western nor Japanese wine. For me it would have to be Kirin lager and Suntory whisky. Gill bought the bottle of gin and some oranges, saying she would improvise. The only other alternative had been the large bottles and barrels of saké.

'Wouldn't touch the stuff, hot or cold,' said Gill. 'Wouldn't touch the oily stuff.'

What were we doing here? Not for the first time, I was asking myself that question. Everyone has a reason for coming to Japan – that's what we used to say. Everyone's escaping from something. There were those for whom it was a flight into an idealized world. They talked as if the place were all Noh plays and pottery villages, geishas and Zen

Buddhist temples, that Japan had retained its authenticity. For them the whole of Japan was a pure invention. They were living in a non-existent country. But we'd come from a non-existent country too.

Just after landing on the island, while Gill was off getting the key, I was waiting by the tiny ferry dock, a cargo coaster now anchored in its bay. A stooped and bald old man was standing, smoking, near me.

'*Amerika-jin, desu ka?*' he asked between drags.

'*Igirisu-jin,*' I replied.

'English gentleman,' he said, in a near unintelligible pronunciation.

'*Arigatō,*' I thanked him.

'I am eighty-eight years old,' he told me in Japanese.

'*Ah sō, desu ka?*' I said.

'*Nihongo wa jōzu desu ne!*' he exclaimed.

My Japanese was perfect. Naturally enough I'd received this compliment before, one only ever given to foreigners who were by no means fluent. The black-hulled coaster with stern bridge and empty holds was turning slightly on its moorings beyond the harbour light. I thanked him again.

'English, gentlemen, Americans, no,' he said. 'We Japanese and English the same.'

'*Sō desu ne,*' I agreed.

Now he was pointing at the sky above the hillock rising behind that moored coaster. It was a clear blue winter's day, a freezing wind blowing, bracingly cold.

'I am too old for the war,' he said. 'I stay here in the war, see American planes in the sky.'

'*Wakarimashita,*' I said. 'I understand.'

'Many many planes,' he said, 'cities all burned.'

'I know,' I said.

'Peace,' he said, 'now, we have peace.'

'I hope so,' I said. He was shaking my hand.

'English gentlemen and Japanese are friends.'

'Friends,' I agreed – as Gill arrived waving the key.

'What was that all about?' she asked as we headed inland.

'He was saying the English are gentlemen,' I said. 'You know, not like the Americans, and all that.'

'It's a point of view,' said Gill.

Yes, a point of view; but one that I didn't disabuse him of, even if I'd been able to try. Admitting to ourselves we must be escaping too, must be suffering from *Europamüdigkeit*, as our German colleagues called it, had been easy enough in principle. Either it had been my mid-life crisis, a way of improving the career prospects by publishing and being damned, or anyway it was a chance to spend more time together and rediscover the bonds in a love that went back to our meeting when still teenagers ourselves. Gill and I would pass the explanations back and forth, sometimes taking up one or the other, depending on which irritation had grated on which of us this time.

These would tend to break out once more around the time of the *bōnenkai*, the year-forgetting parties. This was a tradition I could appreciate. Getting together with the department as the dead zone of the Japanese New Year approached, drinking too much and wiping out the past, could only seem a good idea. Our hiding place for failure, our breeding ground for resentments, the desire for imaginative revenges, the painful labour of regaining control of our lives ... we could put it all behind us, finish the examining and approach the next semester with a wiped-clean whiteboard. But then the sudden drop in temperature, the retirement of the entire native population into their family rituals, the nothing to do but rent another movie – these would turn us in on ourselves in the nowhere of the present, emptily longing for a different future, and blanking out the past, whether recent or from previous lives.

Though there was as little to do on Shiraishijima, we spent the day of New Year's Eve exploring the island with what gusto we could muster. Our first plan was to try and beach-comb all the way round its shores, past the run-down wrecks of boats, shacks and boathouses, kicking through the wrack, with our footprints behind us in the sand.

However, at a certain point the beach gave out into rocks. Round the back of the island, a company was quarrying its cliffs, so we set off inland on a mountain trail to visit the rocky niches where hermit monks would pray. And on one of those bare outcrops of lava from an extinct volcano, I bent down to tie my shoe laces and saw Gill walking on, seeming to leave me behind, though as she turned to find me, with a look of mild irritation on her face, it was as if she were accusing me of hanging back, of letting her go on alone.

Yes, in that dead time of our brief holiday, I was rummaging around in the past for the precise point where it had happened. It wasn't merely that my career had not lived up to expectations. I could have accepted that, had there been compensations. Rather, it was as if I had sacrificed too much for a life that not only wasn't happening, but which now looked as though it could no longer be expected to begin. I had put all my eggs in one basket, nobody wanted to buy them, and now there was precious little left to fall back on. Perhaps it was merely a question of age. Doubtless I was going through a phase.

Then and there I recalled that morning on the Kinki Nippon Railway Station at Nara when I had forgotten myself, forgotten where I was, and tried to kiss Aiko on the cheek. She had shrunk back in horror, and blushed a bright pink. Because she'd been abroad, I thought, it would be a nice gesture to part in the style she would know from her year out in the world. But no, I'd been mistaken. As the train pulled out, Aiko, standing opposite the carriage window, gave a slight bow and disappeared. If attachment to a man depended so largely on the elegance of his leave-taking, it would seem I had managed at a stroke to perform an utterly inelegant parting. But Aiko never so much as mentioned my *faux pas*, and from then on I followed her lead in that too. Doubtless it was another example of the foreigners, drunks and babies rule.

But I could never understand what had made their relationship tick. Other people's feelings were mysteries – you never could see a love affair from the outside, and yet people do sometimes intuit things about other's feelings, even ones concealed from themselves ... They can see the balance of power in a relationship far better, sometimes, than can the protagonists. And there was nothing like someone's death to bring her back to life a while. 'Looking out on the morning rain,' as the song had it. Aiko happened to mention that one once. 'I couldn't face another day ... and when my heart was in the lost and found ...' Yes, that was her favourite song: 'You Make Me Feel Like a Natural Woman' by Carole King, but the Aretha Franklin version. She was so small and, like I say, if she so much as turned sideways you'd think she'd disappear. I used to wonder if she was large enough to bear children. What had the birth of her daughter been like? Don't so much as imagine it. But now Aiko had really disappeared.

It was way past midnight. The picture windows were all of a black, though punctuated here and there by points of light from the mainland. We were standing no more than a few inches from each other, right up at the glass, but weren't about to kiss in that lonely atmosphere. If you'd been lurking in the darkness outside, in the darkness like some peeping Tom, you could have seen us there at the window, lit by a single lamp standing upright in the corner of the room. If you'd been standing in the darkness there, you'd have seen us gesturing with our hands, seen the exasperated expressions on our faces, faces flushed with the rather too much drink from that desultory New Year's Eve. You'd have seen first one and then the other brushing tears from flushed cheeks. Yes, if you'd been standing outside you'd have been able to watch it all like a dumb show, would have seen Gill turn away with one last pained expression. But you wouldn't have heard us say a word.

As so often before, we had stumbled into a line of talk that neither of us planned or exactly expected. Perhaps it was just the drink talking. Or maybe it was the excuse of the drink.

'So why didn't you tell me straight away?' Gill asked, her tone grown harder.

I took a slight step back, but didn't reply.

'Something to hide, eh, Rob?' she asked, taking another swig from her gin and squeezed oranges, and wincing.

'No, not at all, no, why? Should I have?'

'Playing the innocent, as usual,' she said. 'Surely, it's far too late for that.'

'Far too late for what?' I asked.

Gill took a step towards me. Then she leaned forward as if to whisper some tenderness into my ear.

'You've been in love with her all along, haven't you?'

I couldn't help smiling, even if letting out a deep sigh that tasted again of the Suntory whisky.

'Go on, admit it,' she said, fixing me with her inquisitorial gaze.

Had there ever been the shadow of such a possibility? I searched my tired mind for the slightest twinge of guilt that would tell me I was lying – should I so much as deny it there and then. No, I told myself. No, I never loved her. There wasn't the slightest trace of a qualm. But at that very moment, thinking of Aiko once more, just to reassure myself, I found the tears starting again to my eyes. Aiko Mori was dead. But why, why had she done it? What in the world could have happened? How get to such a state of despair that it would seem better to waste all the possible life still left to live?

I was gazing into Gillian's face. My wife was no longer what she'd been when we were young and starting out. That innocent creature was a long time lost. We had been through too much together, the painful and banal, had survived despite it all. But if her innocence is gone, well, so has mine, I thought, while Gill's eyes darkened and her lips parted as if to speak. I saw how my wet face must look, and what it would seem to mean. I turned away as if to catch a sight of ships passing through the dark of night and the darker waters of the Inland Sea. There was nothing but blackness, not even the sound of the waves. I was brushing the moisture from my cheeks as I turned.

'Tears before bedtime!' said Gill with a sickening smile. 'I knew it.'

'No, you didn't and, no, you don't,' I said, my upset about the suicide getting the better of those too volatile feelings for the long-time love and wife who seemed to have taken it upon herself to begin the New Year by tormenting me with my store of regrets. 'I was never in love with Aiko Mori. Do you really think I could be attracted to someone like that? Don't you know me at all? Don't you know yourself?'

'These last couple of months, even when we were in bed, it's like you've hardly been there.' Gill stopped short with her lips slightly parted, as if aghast at what had come through them.

'Look, if I weren't really there, I couldn't even do it!'

But now I did feel a twinge and a qualm. I saw myself lying with my face over the side of the bed, staring blankly at the dusty wood block floor, Gillian speaking all the while. It was so silly. We had relaxed into each other's arms, and dozed for some minutes; then, disentangling, I noticed a small scar to one side of her navel. Not having recalled seeing it before, I asked what it was – which was when she'd decided to tell me. That summer, taking annual leave in England, Gill had missed her period. It was one of those years I came back early to finish correcting the questions for the university entrance exams, and we'd agreed that she would take an extra couple of weeks' vacation before rejoining me in Japan. By the time Gill found she had an ectopic pregnancy, the fertilized egg stuck to the side of one of her fallopian tubes, I was already on the far side of the globe. The doctor explained it would have to be removed, and she would lose one of the tubes. Another pregnancy would be difficult, and might result in complications too. The doctor had suggested that at her age, thirty-seven, she might seriously consider making it impossible for this to happen again. She should talk to her husband.

But she hadn't. She had made the decision herself. It was her body after all. And this was how I found out. I lay there with my head over the side of the bed, continuing to stare at the dusty wooden floor. She knew how much I'd wanted children. She said she thought the lost pregnancy would be too much for me to bear, so the first time we talked she said her doctor had recommended she have the operation, and she'd done it to simplify our sex life. Simplify our sex life! I tried my best to adopt what must be the politically correct attitude. It was her body, and it was her decision. Yet, even as I lay there, it was as if something had been taken from our life together. It was as if we *were* one flesh, and what the doctor had done to her, he had also done to me.

It had been almost two months later, as I lay there unable to get interested, Gill beginning to wonder what had got into me, that she gritted her teeth and told me about the pregnancy – to reassure me about my manhood, she said, but also to give the real justification for her unilateral decision, which of course she couldn't help sensing had upset me. So it had all come out. We had finally, near as damn it, become parents. Not through any decision we'd made, no, but through a mishap. Yet even then it was not to be. The chance of fulfillment had been snatched away as if by some malign fate.

'You've been somewhere else ever since that student of yours died,' said Gill, staring out into the blackness herself.

I was thinking I could make out the lights of a fishing boat afloat in the distance on those waters. Still I couldn't help wondering why my wife had to keep insisting on this implausible fiction to explain the latest of our difficulties.

'No, honestly, no,' I mumbled.

'So why didn't you tell me she'd died as soon as you found out? Why did you keep it to yourself?'

'I was too upset,' I said. 'I didn't know what to think ... and I didn't want to burden you with it as well – when I knew so little.'

'Not that you know any more now,' she said, as if to dispense with that justification. 'Well, anyway, it was obvious to me from the first that she was just all over you. If you hadn't been married, she'd have been doing a Jude and Arabella on you right away, and that's for sure.'

'If you say so,' I said, losing my balance all the time. 'Then why didn't I just ask you for a divorce and run off with Aiko if I was so bloody infatuated?'

'Ah, now he's angry. Now we're getting near the truth.'

The truth, I thought, that would be a fine thing. And then, whether it was the whisky, or the strain of the last few months, or the salt of Aiko Mori's death being rubbed into the wound by Gill's words, an imp of the perverse came out and overwhelmed me.

'All right, all right, I admit it,' I said. 'Oh God, you've dragged it out of me.'

'Tell me, then,' said Gillian, seeming visibly to relax in the knowledge that she had been right all along.

How bizarre to feel such a release in confessing to something that I knew not to be true! Yet in the small hours of that New Year I dipped into the murky sea of my feelings and began to spin a tale of how I'd tried to forget her, had encouraged her connection with Brook to get her out of my life ... and now couldn't help feeling I was somehow to blame for her death.

Which was why all my attempts to keep on the straight and narrow had come to nothing when I discovered she had taken her own life. But why had she done it? Could it have had anything to do with Gillian's jealous intuitions? Now I could only be in love with her memory, it was true, and I couldn't get her out of my mind. And yet as I continued in that vein, it was as if I too felt myself relaxing, as if the idea that I'd been in love with her was the only justification for the extent of those feelings about her death. Why had I become so obsessed with her? No wonder Gillian thought there must have been something going on. It was as if my grief had need of an explanation, and this one fitted it only too well.

'Bet you envied the fact they had a child,' said Gill, as if the least harmful thing would be to have it out then and there – and move on.

'You're probably right,' I said, keeping up the fiction, 'but you did know I wanted to have children, didn't you?'

Which was when the tears had started, uncalled for, into her face too. They came swelling out from around the lashes, making her eyes seem that much larger, making it seem as if the eyes themselves would melt and pour down across her cheeks, before she pulled out a handkerchief and dried them there and then.

What in Heaven's name was I doing? What an idiotic thing to do! Doubtless, Gill had been putting a bold face on the whole business of not having children. She would always say she didn't have the mothering instinct, and didn't see why she should have to fake one – but maybe that was a mark itself of the inner hurt she couldn't address, the hurt expressed in those obviously hapless tears. We stood there silently a moment by the window, wondering where our talk would go to now.

'So what do you propose we do?' said Gillian. 'I can't have children, and you can't have Mori-chan!'

Again, as if looking for inspiration, I turned to the cold glass pane of the window and stared out into the dark waters of the Inland Sea. I was feeling self-pity, it was true, but I was feeling pity for Gill too there beside me – and pitying us both for the death of our love. Yet why did she have to torture me so? And why did I have to torture her in turn? She could give up the pretence of liking Japan. She could go back to England where she belonged. I could keep on with the job I'd got used to, and try to find a life for myself out here ... Why not? It couldn't be worse than this mutually inflicted pain.

'Don't know,' is all I said. 'I don't know.'

'Well, that sounds like the simple truth, for once,' said Gill with the semblance of a smile. 'Why don't we sleep on it and see how things look in the morning?'

'It already is the morning, but I can't wish you happy New Year, now, can I?'

'You don't have to,' Gill said. 'Neither of us can.'

She turned away from the window and walked straight

out through the living room door without so much as a look behind.

So if you'd been standing in the blackness outside the foreigners' holiday hostel, you would have been able to make out clearly that when the woman turned and walked away, the man didn't move for quite a long time. He remained there by the glass just staring out into the darkness. Then, after taking out a handkerchief and wiping his face once more, he turned and walked over to the stereo system positioned against the opposite wall. He picked out a cassette from the three or four lined on the top of one speaker and placed it in the deck. The volume must have been right near the minimum, because you would have seen the man crouch beside one of the speakers. Yes, you would have seen him crouch like that, trying to get some comfort or consolation from the music. But you wouldn't have been able to hear what music it was, and, anyway, out in the darkness of that island on the Inland Sea, there was in fact nobody there.

'What a pleasant coincidence!' said Professor Haneda, as he sat down beside us there at the counter of his favorite haunt.

But this was the last thing I'd wanted to happen. How could I possibly have a quiet talk to Toshi about why Aiko died with Haneda's smiling sybaritic face engaging us in conversation? Assistant Professor Satoshi Miyazaki's favourite watering hole had been closed. So we had descended its darkened stairs and come back out onto Shijo, not far from the Kamogawa bridge. There was nothing else for it but to head for the Department's usual haunt in one of the labyrinthine alleys that formed Kyoto's pleasure district, its Geisha quarter, the Pontochō.

As suggested in my office at the end of his course, I got in touch with Toshi when it emerged we would be stopping overnight in Kyoto on the way back north after our New Year on the Inland Sea. Gill would allow me an evening on the town alone, so I arranged to meet Toshi in the hope of a quiet talk about what had happened. John Frost, the foreign professor at Doshisha University, a friend of mine from those first years in the city, was going to be back home in Chicago for the festive season. He'd offered to let us stay in his traditional-style house on the northwestern flank of the Y-shaped old capital.

'Why didn't Aiko get in touch with someone?' I asked Toshi, rather forlornly, as we made our way through the usual crowds on that very cold, rainy, January evening. 'Why didn't she get in touch with *me*?'

'Not the sort of thing a married Japanese woman could do,' said Toshi. 'I don't suppose she got in touch with you at all once she'd married Brook, did she?'

I had to admit that apart from one New Year card she hadn't. Stepping into the restaurant, Toshi was immediately recognized by the chief sashimi chef. He gestured us towards a couple of seats at the bar's quieter end.

'I hope they weren't living in the house that used to be mine,' I said, remembering waking up one morning that first winter to find the glass of water left beside my futon all but frozen solid.

'They bought a small house soon after they were married,' said Toshi as he refilled my bowl from the dripping hot saké pot. 'But they had also bought some land to build in the country, because Mori-chan was expecting their second ... but then I'm told they were planning to live separately.'

'And why was that?' I asked.

'I hear there was a student ...'

I took another sip of the lukewarm saké.

'Did you ever see the place where she killed herself?' I asked.

'I did not visit them,' he said. 'Brook-san and Mori-chan did not have friends.'

I was about to repeat Professor Sasayama's insight about their ability to form friendships, when Toshi's head of department, Professor Haneda, suddenly pushed through the hanging *noren* before the sliding wooden door. The chief chef, naturally assuming we were all part of the same drinking party, had asked my neighbour to move up one, and the portly professor sat down beside me.

Haneda was a fine old Falstaffian sort of fellow who had invited me along to his teahouse on a couple of memorable occasions those years ago when some visiting writer or other would pass through the old capital. In for a penny in for a pound, I thought, so told Haneda exactly what Toshi and I were discussing, and ended by asking him why he thought the whole thing had happened.

'I'm going to say something that will shock you,' he said.

'I know what it is,' I risked, assuming the liberty taken would be condoned under the foreigners, drunks and babies rule.

'I don't believe there's anything wrong,' Haneda went on, as if I hadn't even opened my mouth, 'with a man having a mistress.'

'Of course, you don't,' I said, putting on my most unshockable tone. 'But you do think there's something wrong with everyone knowing all about it, don't you?'

'Naturally,' the professor came back.

'That's what went wrong when that Australian colla-borator of yours took up with one of his students. He should never have flaunted her around the conference circuit, should he? How could his wife have not found out? You think she shouldn't have made such a fuss? But she hadn't been trained up from birth to play by the Japanese housewife rules. That, you've got to admit.'

'I am sure you felt relieved when your friend Brook came along and took her off your hands,' said Haneda, lifting the saké pot to signal a refill to the restaurant's chief chef.

'Not at all,' I said.

'Ah, so he stole her from you, did he?'

'I don't see how he could have done,' I said, 'seeing as she wasn't mine in the first place!'

'So who's with your wife now? Jack Frost is it?' Haneda came jokingly back with one of his genial smiles, pushing some more deep fried fish-spine into his mouth.

'She caught a cold over New Year,' I said. 'She's gone to bed early.'

Clearly we'd both had sufficient to drink, the rules in abeyance, each overstepping the mark. Toshi was sitting there looking aghast. But why had she done it? Gill's explanation didn't make any sense. I was seeing again the dark windows of the Villa, seeing its stones in their waves of raked gravel. But I was never to see those waters breaking, or embrace the produce of that inland sea.

'Aiko-chan, of course, she used to behave as if she didn't even know what the rules were,' Haneda said, with the smile of a man who had finessed his point.

'But why should you care so much?'

That's what Gill had asked, and come up with her answer.

No, I never was ... but I didn't dislike Aiko as much as some. There were moments when it did seem she had no friends at all. I never heard anyone speak warmly about her. Even her husband appeared to have patronized her. People used to think she was using them. Perhaps she was. But that's not unusual. She may have used me back then, used me to keep up her English. Much good would it do her ... Maybe the difference was I didn't mind being used.

But the Protestant missionaries had. They had appeared to resent the fact that, as they put it, she had been granted the chance to study for a year in Idaho thanks to their good offices; but while she'd been out there Aiko hadn't so much as sent a postcard and, come home, there wasn't even a 'Thank You'. Yet, as far as the missionaries were concerned, she simply hadn't learned the appropriate manners. Nor did this seem to be a question of her faulty English. She didn't seem to know how to behave in Japanese for that matter, when, for example, she was with her professors.

'Ah yes, but then she might well have imagined that being married to an English gentleman, she wouldn't need to know the rules,' I suggested.

'Maybe that was her biggest mistake,' Toshi added in a voice implying that I might refrain from confronting the man with whom he was obliged to work.

'She died for love?' I wondered out loud. 'I mean out of despair?'

'Well,' said Toshi, 'that would be one interpretation.'

'She died because she was too proud to live,' Haneda said with a definitive flourish.

'I take it that's a compliment,' I said.

Haneda called for the bill. He was doing the math, as he'd say. Toshi and I handed over our thirds in the shape of a couple of brown and blue notes.

'Karaoke?' Professor Haneda suggested as we paused at the end of the passage leading from his favourite bar.

I looked across at Miyazaki, dearly hoping to continue our frustrated exchange about what had happened. But Toshi's face said he was caught. He would have to stay on for the sentimental show tunes sung into the small hours.

'I really had better be getting back to my wife,' I said, opting for my usual excuse as we emerged into the rainy neon night.

'Ah, yes, your wife!' said Haneda. 'Very well then, I look

forward to the next time we can do this. It's always good to keep up with the gossip. Goodnight.'

Out in the main thoroughfare, I hailed a taxi.

'*Kitanohakubiya-chō, ni itte kudasi*,' I said.

'*Hakubiya-chō?*' said the taxi driver.

'*Hai*,' I said, and slumped back in the seat.

The Japanese words for *left*, *right*, *straight on*, and *stop* were among the first Aiko had taught me. Since the taxi drivers didn't have anything like 'the knowledge', you had to direct them to where you lived. So, with the aid of those words, and *arigatō gozaimasu*, I managed to have myself deposited just a couple of blocks past the little railway station. The rain was turning to snow as I tried to step out of the taxi and unfurl my umbrella in the same movement, heading off into more narrow dark streets with as much self-possession as I could manage.

So what had become of us all? The persons in their photographs, already dated fashions, people with their *vitaes* of achievements, the vanity mirrors and dental floss, people with birth family bereavements, the ones you had left, or who'd left you, without a backward glance, the others you were pleased to be rid of, the ones you had tried to love? Walking back through the streets of Kyoto past the drinks and pornography dispensers, along the road towards Toji-in, to the house where I'd first visited Jack Frost all those years before, I couldn't help brooding on it all.

So they thought Aiko had married the wrong *gaijin*, the wrong alien, wrong outside-person ... Both Haneda and Gill had said as much.

Jack Frost's house, which Gill and I had been lent for that night, was also traditional, built just after the war, with a single Western-style room. As I approached it from the direction of Toji-in, the narrow pathway through the garden seemed more overgrown than when we had last stayed. It had snowed the night before and even though the ground temperature had risen, melting it all downtown, the air had remained below zero. Cowls of droopy snow, tinged a faint blue in the darkness, remained on the bushes and shrubs. An orange electric bulb glowed above the sliding front door. Showers of refrozen snow, mixed with the freezing rain, tumbled around me as I came up the path towards that familiar silhouette of a one-storey building. I slid the door open and stepped into the *genkan* with its cupboard for shoes on the right.

But just who left that black portable typewriter lying there on the *tatami* floor? Tip-toeing barefoot over towards the darker mound in the back of the *tokonoma* room, still tipsy from that evening's saké, I stumbled right onto its keyboard. A group of silver keys flew up and tried to print their letters onto my freezing cold toes. I failed to repress a yelp of surprise and pain.

'Is that you, Rob?' It was Gill's voice from the direction of that dark mound in the corner.

'Yeah,' I said, then under my breath, 'and who left that bloody old typewriter there?'

Ending up in bed this way, together and alone, I would lie there into the small hours, almost invisible under the futon, not wishing to disturb Gill by cuddling up to her for warmth, everything turning endlessly around in my brain as the drink wore off. The pieces assembled themselves in my head, the story forming from snippets of rumour and gossip. There was no way of knowing how true they were.

'You never can tell,' my old colleague from Chicago had said, 'why someone commits suicide.' Inconstancy, anger, pride and despair ... and I couldn't help picturing her still hanging there, suspended by a twisted scarf from the ceiling, head yanked to one side and arms pulled away from her sides. Brook had found her. He must have collected their daughter from the *hoikuen* after work and taken her back home. He will have tried to get Aiko down, to revive her, take her to the hospital ... but it will have been too late.

'Addicted to picnics,' said Aiko, and so we were, sitting on plastic bags around a tree's roots in the changeable weather of that warm, wet, distant spring. Our heads eye-level with the haze of shifting grasses, new green tints of leafage for the season, two black bikes leaned against a litter basket, drinking beer in the fathomless spaces, serenaded by unidentified bird noise, in the Imperial Palace Gardens, and I certainly remembered this, though nothing here can be trusted to remain the same for long, least of all the tenuous threads that had held us together, not certainly Aiko herself, returning to the place from Idaho and California, who had taken herself so seriously, who had died because she was too proud to live ... And now it was as if I too had grown posthumous to myself, as if I had died and gone into the limbo of those who are in love with the dead.

Yes, I would have to join her on that isle of the dead, on that isle of the dead in the Inland Sea. From its picture window's point of vantage, I could see again across its straits through the fog or mist those red-striped refinery chimneys, the coasters, fishing boats, container ships coming and going like threads extending from our lives. We'd been picking our way across that extinct volcano. She had wrung it out of me, my love. But now as Gill turned over, her face to mine in the *tatami*-scented dark, and I sensed dawn lightening beyond the profile of Mount Hiei, above the Eastern Mountains, it was almost as if that picture window's point of vantage had vanished in a single night.

Indian Summer

Smudged traces of phrases came towards him through the air. The drinkers on the corporation benches were gesturing and talking at each other. Under the canal-side branches, with colours on the turn in that early autumn light, their slurred talk was catching in the leaves – the leaves' lit transparencies, tinting the scene like a stained-glass window. Each mumbled word had a blurred edge to it, and though this made them sound thick or sticky, the joints between felt fragile, like they didn't know where the next one was coming from, or quite where their phrases would end. The two of them seemed clearly to understand each other, or be going through the motions, looking into each other's faces, speaking with an oddly lazy urgency. Passing by, though, he couldn't quite make out what they were saying. He could catch their words, but not the meaning, as happens on the bus when behind two people in the middle of some talk about their lives. All the words were simple enough, but what was the story? The snippets of talk wouldn't form into a shape with a background, a point, or an end in sight.

Then as he came closer, the drinkers on the benches turned out to be women, women of uncertain age, younger, probably, than he would have thought. They could have been homeless, sleeping rough, making the most of the only season when that might seem an alternative to the warmth and shelter most took for granted. He thought how the drink might numb the cold in winter, or it would help the days slide by at any time of year. Both of them clutched an open can of lager, their other hands gesturing broadly as if to help the words come out, like a conductor with an orchestra in a first-time rehearsal of some piece. The flushed-faced women were mottled all over with a warm glow from the oblique rays separated out by that colander of shade formed in the canal-side leaves.

The day had thoroughly warmed itself through. Light was gleaming brilliantly across the flowing water, dazzling anyone not wearing sunglasses on such an October day. It had been hotter for the season than at any time since records began, or so the media forecasters put it. Perhaps the climate was changing, just as they said, for the better or worse. On the canal – the canalized river – were pairs of swans floating in parallel with the couples that strolled the towpath on their way to town. The lapping water murmured along between banks, following its track past flats and office blocks, in its own valley of human habitation, whispering like a tributary under sleep, bringing clearer notes to air and distance, out of sight most of the time, forgotten about, but on days like these a blaze of light in the midst of life, forming what you might call a point of repair.

Down the canal-side came the crowds of unknowing, in twos and threes, mothers and babies, foreign languages and accents, the mysteries in lives that are paid so little attention as they pass, and the fear of each other in their differences, the minimal eye-contact, the checking of appearances. It was all like that slight anxiety produced by the sound of the two drunk women on the corporation benches, as if their out-of-focus speech would ruin the mellowed clarity of light, the brightness on the water, this cloudless blue above the town's transformed industrial quarter.

But for him this warmth and clarity had its own precarious aspect, its own premonition of a possible disaster. But there was no need to exaggerate. The worst it could be was a mild disappointment. He knew well enough how it sometimes is when you meet up with a person after many, many years. Perhaps that's why most people let their pasts go. They dread the thought of meeting somebody who might be holding one of their old selves hostage, or they don't want to revisit the reasons that made them lose touch in the first place. Daunted, those selves would reappear as from cavernous oubliettes – no, not as they were, but with the damage of the years quite clear on their faces, in words, nervous laughter, or looks in blinks of eyes. Staring right ahead, he could see it happening over again in the faint shade of the leaves' lit transparencies, towards twilight on the last day of their working week, a Friday that had thoroughly warmed itself through.

And for a moment he was taken aback by this familiar post-industrial scene, the whole warmed-through array lacking any kind of focus, or sense of direction, notwithstanding the canal-bank walk, the distant car noise, or life's dispersive forces; he could sense the scene those drinkers saw and hear what they had seemed to say aright: that its leaves were spring blossoms, the warmth like a June night's, though earlier. And here again were the empty office spaces flanking each side of the waterway by which he was walking, walking once more on an autumn day that might have been forming a point of repair, one of those moments when mind and world can seem to coincide.

She had sent him a message with her mobile number on it. They had met at one of those unforeseen reunions, one of those funerals when a contemporary finds sudden death in the midst of life. In fact almost a year had gone by since that bitter winter's day in a crematorium at the far end of the country, when he'd seen her again for the first time in years, so many years, and such interrupting circumstances, after they had gone their separate ways.

But how strange it was after all those years that they should find themselves living in the same town, on opposite sides of the cemetery, about a five-hour drive from where they grew up, more than thirty years after they had fallen out of touch. And, unexpectedly too, she'd suggested they meet and have a drink after work for old time's sake. Her husband would be looking after the evening meal, as he did most of the cooking, and her kids were old enough to look after themselves. No, it wouldn't be a problem – as she said – he needn't worry.

~

But he did worry, and was far too early as usual, approaching the central station where they'd agreed to meet with more than half an hour in hand. So he ducked into an Oxfam bookshop just to while away the time.

'What an Indian summer's day!' the lady on the cash register exclaimed, and he managed a word of sociable agreement.

Running his eye along the cracked spines and titles, mentally ticking off which ones he'd read already, his mind kept returning, as it had for weeks on end now, to those sticky moments more than thirty years before. It had all begun at a Christmas party in an underground club by the waterfront. Down the bottom of the stairs from street level was a cavernous room with a bar, some tables and chairs, a jukebox, and space for dancing. Someone had organized the party, he couldn't remember who, and the place had been booked sight-unseen, which was a pity because it felt far too big for the gang of friends from twinned boys' and girls' schools in the suburbs. They were a strangely shy lot, really, meeting like that each weekend to pass the difficult years of teenage together, but hardly talking or getting to know each other better. They would sip drinks and listen to music, talk about bands and new releases ...

The girls would like to do some dancing, and had started choosing disco records on the jukebox, as if to give those boys the hint. When they didn't take it the girls would start to dance with each other anyway. Then, having drunk enough to take the edge off their inhibitions, the boys too would do some rhythmical shuffling about on the floor, making the minimal movements compatible with not losing the beat or their cool. The appropriate way to manage this was to be in the vicinity of a girl, so they would sort of pair off in such a fashion as not to let it be allowed to mean a thing.

That evening, though, the day before Christmas Eve, a little more drink in him than would seem for the best, he found himself doing the jerk, as it were, in her vicinity. It wasn't entirely an accident, of course. She was the one he had always felt himself most inclined towards. She was small-featured and pretty; she was shy, with cheerfully modest, unselfconfident laughter ... She could dance well too, so much more at ease in her movements than she seemed when sitting in the midst of their talk, to which she would rarely contribute.

The dance music came to an end and another song started, a little slower. He had stopped dancing; she was there in front of him. But he was in a dither about whether to go on or sit down. And so, it seemed, was she. They looked into each other's faces as if to get some guidance as to what should happen next. That was when it happened, unplanned, unexpected, unexplained. They both moved towards each other and, the music being slower, both reached out their arms; but instead of doing some more smoochy dancing they took hold of each other and started to kiss – not a brief kiss, but a long passionate one, holding each other firmly in their arms. And it had that feeling of immense relief when something finally gets expressed, as if something that everyone knows has finally been said. Yet, at the same time, they were both taken wholly by surprise at what had happened, and so, as was clear when they stopped, were the friends of both sexes round about them.

That kiss had been such a definitive statement, like one of intent that had not been intended. When they stopped and looked into each other's faces once again, it was as if they would now have to do that much harder thing. They would have to invent a way of being together, of talking to each other like a couple, to turn their evidently mutual attraction into voices sounding together, paying the peculiar attention to each other that boy- and girlfriends do. She had left a half-finished drink on one of the tables, so took him by the hand and led them back to where she'd been sitting with her friends ...

Over the next six months or so, they would meet on their own or together with the others. Sunday afternoons would be spent in the room built out above her parents' garage, putting the records on, speculating a bit about others' intrigues, snuggling up on the sofa together. And just as in the comedies everyone's seen, her mother would of course come in and find them rapidly disentangling themselves. They certainly saw a few romantic films together, ones she and her best friend had invited him along to, and, however little he wanted to see them, he'd gone to be with her and then found himself caught up in the tearful movies too.

Yet despite his aching affection for her, the warmth of her attraction, he still couldn't help feeling guilty about those afternoons and evenings in the music room above their garage. He had wanted to touch and kiss every part of her, and tried his best to do just that. Being a teenage boy, and looking back on it, all he could sense was the years of frustration, the shame of declarations made to entirely uninterested girls, the embarrassments of wanting too much, too much or sometimes too little. The terrible silences walking out with girls you fancied, through cemeteries and down canal-bank walks, the sudden and wholly unexplained breakings off or harsh words said, they had all been so acutely painful. But the thought of how he had hurt other people was worse, and she was one of the ones he had hurt.

But most of all, eyes half-focused now on the rows of second-hand books, his mind went back to one strange day towards that summer's end, the summer he worked as a night watchman in a dressmakers' mannequin factory up on the estate ... He would walk back from the lodge at its gates, down the empty dawn boulevard home, then tumble into bed for a night's sleep in the daylight. It was a strange kind of half-life. He would wake in the late afternoon and have breakfast, watch the early evening news, get his sandwiches and reading matter ready, packing them into his faded canvas army surplus gas-mask bag, then head back up the road for another long nightshift.

But that day in late August all those years ago the gang had phoned after he'd only been asleep for two or three hours. He staggered downstairs at the sound of mother calling, picked up the great black Bakelite receiver, and listened to the voice at the end of the line. It came to him out of an interrupted dream. His friends were driving down the coast to their nearby seaside resort and would he like to come along too? He wondered had she suggested it? Yes, she was coming with some of her friends, and, despite the difficulty meeting as things stood, since they still were sort of together, maybe she had wanted him along. There was just enough time for him to throw on some clothes and shave before there they were, turning up at the door with a parent's borrowed car to pick him up and go.

Thrown together by the centrifugal force of the swing-boat's flying cars on that chilly summer's day, they both took advantage of the fairground attraction's usual excuses for clinging on to each other, clinging with all their might. And it came back to him there, as he picked out a green murder mystery, scanned the first few sentences and replaced it on the shelf, that this had been their moment of nearest intimacy, of their being wedged together, flying in a spaceship through the onshore breeze, nearer than ever they'd been on that sofa above the garage, with the distances reduced to a dream-like nothing in his sleep-deprived state, with his arm around her shoulder in all the exhilaration of that movement through the air, even though the forces were gathering already, the forces that would soon prise them apart.

❧

Then there she was, suddenly, as if formed out of scraps in the crowd. There she was by the exit where he waited, another stranger but for the look of recognition, and her coming straight towards him with a smile on her much changed face. Time had, of course, wrought its changes on them both. They were more rounded than in youth, more firmly defined, whether from illness, parenthood, or the world of work. Yet there were her small feet and hands, her carefully picked-out clothes, and that certain recognition in the warmth of eyes and lips. And he was leaning forward to give her a peck on each cheek, European-fashion – not something he'd have dreamt of when they were young together.

A Friday it was, at the end of another working week, the bars around the station concourse filling up with people who were winding down and fuelling up. This wasn't something he could do any more, time and illness leaving him with a far too fragile constitution for the exertions that those round them seemed intent on as they entered one of those vast drinking barns, the bare floorboards and tables constellated with ring-stains of glasses. They had found themselves an unoccupied table after buying a drink at the bar.

When he'd tried to get close to her, all those years before, she was very svelte, with a childlike simplicity of look, but an edge of perceptiveness about what was going on around her that could easily be missed in her modest, calm demeanour. They had both put on weight, his explanation being a changed metabolism and his sedentary trade, hers the having children, and an illness that had left her bedridden for some months, after which she'd not been able to recover her previous shape. Her face too had filled out, but it was soft still and largely unlined, entirely free of those marks of weakness and woe that can scour with the burden of the years.

They filled in their accounts of what had brought them by such circuitous routes to be living in the same town, after all the years of their separate wanderings. Her first marriage had failed, her second husband a victim of cancer, but now she was with the kindest man, had been with him for decades. It was with him that she had had her children. He, on the other hand, he had never settled, had lived abroad for many years, had sacrificed his life to the career. No, he had never married.

She told him how she'd come to be working for an environmental agency simply because they were short-handed one week and, after helping them out, they had asked her to stay on. She explained this with the unembarrassed incredulity that anyone could ever find anything of value in her. No, not fishing for compliments, she didn't seem to have a low opinion of herself, in the sense that her modesty didn't seem a form of self-humiliation. Of course, he said how they wouldn't have kept her on if they hadn't seen her value to the operation; but she clearly didn't need any reassurance either.

Then there were her children's educations, and her other half's problems in the current labour market. They skated over mortgages, shared fears of negative equity – the usual topics, in other words. She was expecting to sell their house when the time came to downsize, and to pay off their debts into the bargain. They had, she admitted, been living a little beyond their means.

'But it's only money,' she said with a smile.

She had placed her mobile on the table beside her almost empty glass. It began to make one of those curious buzzing noises. This was her daughter phoning about some arrangements or other. So he tuned out of what she was saying into the mobile, letting the undifferentiated hubbub of the drinkers around them wash over his dreaming head.

'They don't seem to have any mystery in their lives,' she said, putting the mobile back beside her glass.

'I mean,' she continued after he'd asked, 'the way they put up what they're feeling so directly on those social network sites ... They don't seem to allow even the slightest shred of mystery in their relationships any more. Everything's so up front and out in the open. I mean the way people talk about their most intimate experiences walking through a shopping mall or in a crowded carriage ... It's not the privacy violated,' she said, 'but the loss of all the mystery in what others think or feel ... which, I suppose,' she continued, 'is a kind of fear of others ... but a good fear, like a kind of admiration,' she said, and he couldn't help agreeing, looking around at the people chatting, ones texting, calling orders, phoning others who would meet up with them later ...

'So do you think we had more, back then?' he asked her.

'I never knew what anyone was thinking,' she said, 'and especially you.'

He gave her what he hoped was a modestly incredulous look.

'I mean, you were so musical and sensitive,' she said. 'I always felt in awe of you.'

'Really,' he said, 'is that really what you thought?'

'We all did.' That's what she said.

'Well, I never knew,' he said, and wondered what it meant.

Neither said anything more for a moment, but looked around that noisy bar again. And he couldn't help noticing that they seemed the oldest people in the place. He was letting her words sink in, turning his head to catch a glimpse of the side of her face, she instantly meeting his eyes. For it seemed that not only did he not need to be forgiven, it seemed he had never done her any harm at all.

Astonishment, gratitude, relief appeared; and there was well-being in the autumn leaves as they walked out in the cooler air and parted at the station, she to catch her bus and he to take the canal-bank walk once more. She had left him with her parting embrace, her warmly unequivocal arms, her arms around him again after many, after so many years.

❧

But as he passed by the weeping willow trees, their pendant fronds pointing back up at him from the sluggish, filmed water beyond that black wrought-iron bridge, he realized he'd not said how he felt about *her*. Now that he was walking back to the other part of town, his side of the cemetery, the amber lights beside the canal glowing in the multiple reflections, the dark, the surviving factory buildings, he couldn't help reflecting on the changes all around. He had always liked this part of town, with its mossy lock gates and old gasometer, the waterside pubs, ducks, swans, and mooring posts. Anything like that could remind him of his childhood, his teenage entanglements, and, among them, the interrupted year that they had shared. And to think she hadn't even needed to forgive him! No, he'd not been able to tell her how grateful he was; and she would have surely not envisaged him being so after all those years.

That corner of a person he had never been, the one who felt guilty about how he'd treated her, the one he had lived with all this time, she had abolished it with her generous words. It was like being given back a bit of your integrity, something he had lost, or had been taken from him, somewhere down the way. That was what other people could do; they could restore, could repair some things of you. It was what she had done, even if unawares.

Nor had it felt as if they were responding to each other as they had back then. How could they have done, two middle-aged people with their different lives, their different sets of fates? That was quite impossible. They were not the same as they had been, not the young people in the entrance to adulthood, experimenting with what might be felt and done. Of course they couldn't be as they had been. Even a modicum of respect for the experiences each had undergone, and recognition of the relationships that these had given rise to, would have made them accept each other's weight in the world. It was what they had acknowledged in effect as they talked and sipped their drinks for an hour or so of warmth on that unusually warm, that Indian summer's day.

And she had been quite different, had not been at all how he remembered or imagined her. Oh but then she'd made him feel quite different too – and in that she was also still the same.

Two Rivers Press has been publishing in and about Reading since 1994. Founded by the artist Peter Hay (1951–2003), the press continues to delight readers, local and further afield, with its varied list of individually designed, thought-provoking books.